Mafia Secrets

Vi Carter

WARNING

This book is a dark romance. This book contains scenes that may be triggering to some readers and should be read by those only 18 or older.

NEWSLETTER

Join my newsletter and never miss a new release or giveaway.

CHAPTER ONE

O'REAGAN
AN CHLANN

DANIEL

The buzz of excitement brushes against me as I stand in the corner of my new club. It settles on my skin but never seems to infiltrate my system like it does to others as they dance, talk, and have their fill of drink. I have no idea what it would take for me to feel something close to excitement.

I step away from the shadows that had wrapped around me and walk onto the red carpet, which runs down the center of the room. Small wooden dividers break the room into four. Plants placed in very specific areas give the patrons the illusion of privacy, but our cameras and security have full coverage. We aren't keeping a watch on their sinful play; I don't care who screws who. It's the small drug dealings that go down in our clubs that we won't allow. That's my business, and anyone stupid enough to walk into an O'Reagan club and deal right under our noses deserves to be punished. I like to remove a finger; it's my trademark, my warning, my trophy for wiping anyone out who would dare stand against us.

To stand against an O'Reagan is a suicide mission, but I do come across stupid boys who want to meet their maker quickly because they think money makes them men.

All eyes are on me; everyone here knows who I am. And who am I? I'm an O'Reagan, of the east Mafia of Ireland. I hadn't always known who I was, but even when I was young, I knew I belonged to something bigger. Crime was something I fell into even at school, behind the lockers making quick money from drugs or illegal cigarettes. I always had a knack for it.

Dolores, a fifty-year-old woman who lived a few doors away from us, flew to Turkey several times a year. She was our mule for illegal cigarettes, and I took every pack she supplied me and made a good profit from it. I often look back on those days with fondness, the hustle of it all. The adrenaline of wondering if I'll get caught. I did — more times than I can count. My mother tried to beat the badness out of me, but once you have a taste for money, there is no going back.

It wasn't until I was in my twenties that I discovered why crime, violence, and quick money was in my blood. I never knew my father or what family I belonged to. My life was a lie until my father died, and in his will, he named me and my brother as his only heirs.

I watch as my cousin Shay steps into the club, cigarette in hand, completely at ease in his t-shirt and jeans, as his gaze sweeps across the room. He gives no fucks about the dress code as he stands among men dressed in suits. Shay's wild eyes finally land on me as he takes a long draw on his cigarette before walking in my direction.

"This is a no-smoking premise," I remind him while I keep an eye on everyone as Shay joins me.

"I'll take it up with management," Shay grins and takes another drag of his cigarette.

Everyone watches us; if they didn't know who Shay O'Reagan was before tonight, they will now. Groups of patrons huddle together, whispering as their gazes keep swinging back to Shay and me. Their gazes divert when they meet my eyes, none of them bold enough to hold my stare. I know our clubs are full of young men wanting to get a glimpse of the Irish Mafia in hopes they can rub shoulders with us and maybe get a job. But, not many are brave enough to approach us.

"Darragh was here yesterday, and I already said no." I know Shay is a king, and saying no to him really isn't an option. If they want to turn my establishment into a whore house, I can't stop them, but that doesn't mean I'll roll on my back and let them tickle my balls.

Shay walks to a table that's recently been vacated and drops his cigarette into a half-empty glass. He's facing me now. Scratching his beard, he takes a look around him before his gaze settles on me again. My spine straightens. Something isn't right. I don't see Shay much, and I never get a personal audience with him. Normally, I only talk with him when all the O'Reagans come together.

"This is your establishment. Do what you want with it." Shay offers, and his word is final. I won't have to do what Darragh asks.

I nod, but I feel no relief as I wait for the blow of why Shay O'Reagan is here.

"The club in Athboy was attacked."

Fuck.

"Is it bad?" I ask.

Shay nods and takes out his phone. The screen is lit up, and Emma's name flashes across. Shay pockets his phone without taking the call from his wife. I'm sure she won't have to wait long as his stance changes like he's ready to flee. It's odd to see Shay dance to someone else's tune as he's only ever danced to his own, that is, until he met Emma.

She's the only person in the world that has Shay's complete respect.

"Jack was already over there. He got a name. Mike McGuinness. We have men hunting him already."

My system seems to be flooded with ice when hearing that name. McGuinness.

Shay takes out his phone. "I better go. I just thought I should tell you in person."

I track Shay as he slips from the club; the last thing I see him do is raise the phone to his ear. McGuinness. What are the odds?

It's been over three years since I've uttered that name and swore to destroy her. Lily McGuinness, the girl who tore my fucking heart out. She fucked me over and left me without a backward glance, and now her uncle is attacking my businesses.

I walk deeper into my club, my mind reeling with memories of Lily: Her smiling brown eyes, she had looked at me like I was a god. She had made me feel like one. I had the pleasure of kissing every inch of her tanned skin until she broke up with me and left.

Even after I buried my father and laid my brother to rest, Lily's betrayal was like a numbing gel, and fuck me, she had lathered it on thick. Feeling anything these days was hard, all because of her, and now her uncle had the balls to touch what is mine.

More people pour into the club, they move around me, but I sense their stares. I can't make out their whispered words, but I know they speak of me. Another flood of people enters, and my eyes lock on one. She's smiling; she's older, she's more womanly.

Lily.

CHAPTER TWO

O'REAGAN
AN CHLANN

LILY

I find myself at Club Forty-Seven with my work colleagues. I'd rather be at home by the fire with a glass of Prosecco and a good book. But I'm trying to be more sociable. My mother says I would put an introvert to shame with how much of a recluse I am. A new-born nun she often teases. I don't find her words funny. I wasn't always like this.

No. My mother and her brother did this to me.

"What can I get you, Lills?" My coworker Jonathan asks. He's sweet, caring, and I know he sees more than just a work colleague when he looks at me. I've made it clear nothing will happen between us, and Jonathan agrees, but at moments like this, I cringe at the want in his soft green eyes.

"Just juice." I shrug out of my heavy black jacket. My work suit underneath is too professional for this club. I'm trying not to look around at all the half-naked women that seem to float around. I'm only twenty-one, but I feel old and frumpy. I'm tempted to pull out the band that keeps my hair tied back and free my long brown hair. But what would the point be? I'm not trying to impress anyone.

"Black currant or orange?" Jonathan asks. Most people laugh when I say juice, not Jonathan. Sometimes that makes this worse.

I stop looking into his green eyes. "Black currant." I slide into a chair across from Laura and Crystal. We all work in the same accounting office in town.

"This place is deadly." Crystal is practically bouncing on the red cushioned couch that runs along the wall. Large mirrors over her head allow me to see the club behind us. I pick up a beer mat and play with it feeling all sorts of awkward. A shiver runs across my neck and tightens my shoulder blades, and I get the sense I'm being watched, but I don't dare look over my shoulder. No doubt Jonathan is watching me from the bar.

"You are going to break his heart," Crystal says, like she can read my mind.

"I already told him where we stand," I confess and stop fidgeting. I'm not one to shy away from awkward conversations. I don't like them, but I also won't run. I've spent most of my life running, and I've lost too much already.

"You need to tell him again, girl." Crystal is grinning, her red lips stretch across snow-white teeth. She's beautiful and brave with her candy-pink hair. I always admire how she just goes for it. No apologies.

"Here you go, Lills." Jonathan places the drink in front of me. I touch the black straw, pausing before I take a drink. The sense of being watched makes me hyper-aware of my surroundings.

"I can't believe Kelly picked you two to go back to England. You are so fucking lucky," Kieran pipes up. I would gladly give up my spot. Traveling back to England, even if it's for a weekend, is the last thing I want to do. But it's the final part of my training, and then I'll be a qualified chartered accountant. I enjoy my job. I don't love it. But I enjoy it. It affords me a sense of solitude and honest living. One that keeps me far away from my family's underhanded dealings.

I shift uncomfortably in the chair at the thoughts of my family. My God, I just want to go back to my house and lock the door.

I take a sip of the juice. Kieran says something to Crystal that has her laughing. Laura's checking her phone, and I take a peek at Jonathan to find him watching me.

"Is your drink okay?" he asks.

"No, the black currant is too black currant. What the fuck, Jonathan." Kieran spouts before rolling his eyes. "She's not going to fuck you."

I die a little inside. I like them, I do. But they are just acquaintances, and all of a sudden, I'm wondering what I am doing here.

"Don't be so mean, Kieran." Laura tries to defend Jonathan, and I know if anyone will get through to Kieran, it's Laura.

"You're so rude. We are just friends." Jonathan's lame words make me cringe.

But I don't want to leave him hanging. So I force a smile. "We are all friends," I say. I try so hard to fit in, to hide my own nature. To hide who I am. I don't want anyone to look down on me, but honestly, I wouldn't blame them.

A dark figure catches my eye in the mirror, and the black currant juice becomes bitter on my tongue. The blood seems to freeze in my veins, and I'm rising from my seat. It can't be. I spin around, and my heart hammers as I glance over the crowd. But the dark figure is gone. I had thought I saw Daniel, only he was more-terrifying looking than I remember. Even with his light blue eyes and blond hair, Daniel had such a darkness in him.

A hand circles my wrist. "Are you okay?" Jonathan's concern has me shaking off the sense of dread. I had thought I had seen Daniel, the boy who destroyed me. I have never loved anyone like I loved him. I know I never will, but he was the wrong kind of love.

I was obsessed with him. They say he was obsessed with me. An obsession that I would have gladly stayed in.

"Yeah, I thought I saw someone." I slowly sit back down. His name suited him, a god. That's how I often saw him.

"You look like you saw a ghost." Crystal leans across, her cleavage almost spilling out of her silver top. Crystal and Laura both had gotten changed at the office before we came here, so I stood out a mile and even more so now, with how awkward everything feels.

"Not a ghost," I finally answer Crystal. I would never compare Daniel to a ghost. He was so present. He was a presence that everyone was aware of. He made you want to impress him. You wanted his attention, but often when I had it, it was too much. He was too much. Too intense, too dark. I pick up the glass and take a long drink through the black straw. "Yeah, it was someone from high school." I never speak about my past, and I can see even Kieran is paying attention to me. "A friend," I say while they all stare at me.

Crystal waggles her eyebrows. "A friend with benefits?"

She wrestles a slight smile out of me. It was so much more than that. Daniel was everything. Sounds stupid, but I can't explain how he was my every thought and breath, all that mattered was me and him. I take another drink, but no matter how much I gulp it down, it doesn't stop the dryness that's closing my throat.

I drain the glass. "Just a friend," I answer Crystal. Kieran and Laura are leaning back into the couch and talking across Crystal. They smile at each other, and I wonder when they will admit their feelings. I don't dare look at Jonathan. I know he most likely is staring at me.

"I'm going to get a drink." I rise and turn with the empty glass in my hand, only to freeze.

"Daniel," I say his name in a terrified breath. Because that's what he is at this very moment. Terrifying.

CHAPTER THREE

O'REAGAN
AN CHLANN

DANIEL

She's here in front of me. If I reached out, I could touch her face.

"Lily McGuinness. What do I owe you for this pleasure?" I smirk.

Her cheeks flood with color as she glances at her friends, who are gawking with no shame. "I don't go by that name." Her words are low and clipped, but even over the music, I hear them.

I step closer and inhale her scent openly.

Her eyes widen.

"You are still wearing Daisy?" That was her favorite perfume.

"I go by the name Lily Rodgers." She bristles.

I let my grin widen. "Do you now?" I glance down at her friends. "Are you married?" The thought sends me almost spiraling. Who the fuck is he? Who do I have to kill?

The pulse flickers in her neck, and her eyes plead with me.

I wouldn't give two fucks if she was on her knees with my cock in her mouth; I'd still want to destroy whoever touched what is mine.

I wave my finger at her. "Is he at this table?"

She shakes her head; her long slim fingers tighten around the glass. Hands that had caressed my body and given me so much pleasure. My gaze skips to her lips, and my mind is flooded with everything she did with her mouth. I want to shift as my cock starts to grow.

"I'm not married. It's my mother's maiden name."

Too much relief wipes out the murderous thoughts of only seconds ago. How can she flip a switch inside me? She always had the ability. I didn't think after three years, she could hold such power, but she still does. I have more control now, and I won't let her know that. So I grin and stare at her.

She bites her lower lip before shrugging; each rushed breath she inhales reminds me of a drowning fish. She has no idea how to process this moment. I could help her out, but this is too much fucking fun.

"I heard you fucked off to England."

She grits her teeth. "Please, don't." Her gaze turns watery, and my temper flairs. She left me, she broke my fucking heart, and she's looking at me like I did her wrong. Typical fucking woman. Always the victim.

I'm ready to continue when one of my security men touches my shoulder. I reel in my anger and glance at him. "Darragh is here to see you, sir."

I face Lily, who looks ready to cry. "The drinks are on me."

"For the table," I tell my security.

"No." Lily yelps as I walk away from her. I wonder how it feels to see my back and wonder if this is the last time she will ever see me. It should be the last time. I need to cut her off, but that's not going to happen. I already feel it. I need to punish her for what she did to me. And her uncle attacking my business gives me a good reason to keep an eye on her. I couldn't reach her when she skipped off to England, but she's back now, and I will make it my business to destroy Lily.

Darragh is in the VIP area with a bottle of champagne. He's my father's twin brother, and I inherited their blue eyes and blond hair.

"The devil dressed like a god," Darragh says the minute I arrive. This is a line he often greets me with. I would normally brush off the comment, but I'm not in the mood today.

"I would beg to differ, Darragh. I'm sure in your lifetime you've done some bad shit."

Darragh grins and lights up a cigarette. He knows this is a non-smoking establishment, but the O'Reagans don't follow the rules.

He offers me one, and I decline.

"You hear about the club in Athboy?" Darragh asks while pouring himself a glass of champagne.

I try to relax in the seat. I can't see Lily's table from this angle. "Yeah, Shay was here."

"Fuck's sake. He could have said and saved me a trip." Darragh takes a long sip of champagne.

"You don't look too put out," I remark.

"I am a man who sees an opportunity in everything he does."

I turn to Darragh. "Jack found out it was Mike McGuiness."

Darragh nods. "I heard that too. I have my boys tracking him."

"Any news yet?" I ask.

Darragh shakes his head before taking a long drag of his cigarette. “Nope. But I’m sure it will be soon.”

I sit forward on the couch. “I’ll leave you to enjoy your champagne.”

I rise.

“Did you think about my other offer?”

I look down at Darragh. “I’m going to decline.” I wasn’t turning any of my clubs into a backdoor whore house.

Darragh shrugs. “A pity. You are leaving money on the table.”

“I’ll find another way; I always do.” Money comes easily to me. That’s the mantra I tell myself, and it has worked my entire life.

I walk to the red rope that stops people from walking into the VIP area. Lily is waiting for me with her arms folded. She’s arguing with one of my security guards. When she senses me looking at her, she glances and swallows all her words. I could tell my security to get rid of her.

I unclip the rope and place it back in the hook as I move down the steps.

“I told her to go away, boss.” My security informs me.

I hold up a hand. “It’s fine.” I pin Lily with a stare. “What do you want?”

She folds her arms across her generous bust. “I don’t know.”

I walk toward her and stop so we are shoulder to shoulder. I’m a good foot taller, so I lean down and whisper in her ear. “Don’t play with me, Lily.”

“I’m not.” I meet her gaze before I glance at her lips.

My cock twitches.

I straighten and nod toward the back, where I have a private room. I grin when she hesitates and give her a look that says I’m laughing at her.

I walk away and toward the dark mahogany door that has a gold plaque with the word private engraved on it.

I push open the door, and I can smell Lily before I turn and look down at her.

"Ladies first." I hold the door open.

She swallows and steps into the lion's den.

CHAPTER FOUR

O'REAGAN
AN CHLANN

LILY

The room that Daniel takes me to has that fresh smell of newness that's carried throughout the club. As he closes the door behind me, the noise of the club vanishes along with my courage. I'm wondering what I am doing here, but I know it's Daniel. He walks to a desk but doesn't sit behind it; instead, he leans against the large, heavy oak table and folds his arms. He appears formidable. His gaze holds nothing but boredom, and I'd question if he even remembered me; only he had used my name outside in front of my friends.

Right now, he appears bored. "I didn't know this was your club," I say, self-conscious of my appearance. I'm tempted to run my hand across my ponytail or straighten my suit jacket.

"If you had known, would you have come?" He questions. His voice rumbles across my flesh. He's still Daniel, just older, more good looking, if that's even possible. His blue eyes always had the power to make me feel like I was the only person in the world that he saw. I glance away as a million emotions rush through me all at once. His question should have a simple answer, like yes or no, but would I have come with friends if I had known this was his club?

"I don't know," I say and sound pathetic.

He unfolds his arms and tilts his head like I'm something to be examined under a microscope.

"I don't want your drinks." I find myself saying. I glance at the paintings that hang on the wall. The scenes are of pure Irish beauty. The wilderness, the landscape, the barren green fields. None of them match the dark soul that takes a step toward me.

"Then don't drink them. But..." He grins like he knows something I don't. "Your friends seem to be enjoying them."

He's right; everyone is enjoying their free drinks and talking about who Daniel is. Crystal is already besotted. When she said he was dreamy in a dark and untouchable kind of way, I wanted her to stop. She had no right to look at him like that. I had no right to feel so protective over him, to be fair. It's been years since we saw each other.

Johnathan was the only person who refused the drink. I don't know if it's because of how stiff I became after Daniel left.

"So, what do you want?" Daniel asks and takes a step toward me.

What do I want? I don't know. I wanted to see if he was still the same person I left behind. Not a night passed when I didn't think about him. "I...." I frown and fold my arms over my chest even as Daniel continues to advance toward me. He stops walking, towering above me like some looming god. A part of me is giddy, but another part tells me to stop this, to leave and return to my friends. There is so much to say, but as I look into Daniel's gaze, I wonder if he even cared that I left or if he easily moved on to another girl. He had so many admirers that I knew he wouldn't be alone, not for a second.

"I just wanted to thank you for the drinks but also to say that we are fine." I sound so stupid.

A shiver starts at the base of my spine and dances in swirls all the way to my neck as Daniel reaches out; one finger touches my cheek, stealing any air that remains in my lungs. I'm tempted to close my eyes; his touch feels like home. It's a touch I've yearned for. His cologne circles me. As his gaze slides across my face and pierces through my flesh, it worms its way around my heart, causing my pulse to beat rapidly. I'm tempted to rip the watch off my wrist that tracks my heart rate. What if it starts to beep with my erratic beats?

"That's all I wanted to say." I pivot and try to take calm steps to the door. He doesn't stop me, and when I open the door, sound comes crashing back in, and it's like stepping into another world. A world without Daniel. I pause at the door, the urge to turn around and explain everything to him. But he isn't asking any questions, so this is just a one-way thing. Me not letting him go. He obviously has moved on and up in the world. I close the door, and each step is heavy as I move across the club. A few people are dancing. When Johnathon appears in front of me, it pulls me back to the present.

"Dance with me?" he asks.

I'm startled by his request and also the exchange I just had with Daniel. I find myself being swept onto the dance floor. The music isn't particularly slow, but Jonathan places his hand on my hip, the other curls around my back, and I let him lead me. I'm not much of a dancer, but I'm so aware of everything around me. Jonathan's hands should make me feel something, but that one finger that Daniel touched me with had such an impact. I find myself reaching up and touching my cheek.

"Are you okay?" Jonathan asks, and I realize I've stopped dancing.

No. I'm not okay. I'm pining over a boy whom I loved, whom I never stopped loving. I had expected Daniel to follow me to England, to find me and take me back where I belonged with him. Even as a young man, he wielded more power than my uncle. He could have gotten me back if he wanted me.

He didn't. I remind myself. I'm being stupid. I know that. But, being here in his club, with his scent still so vivid in my memory, it's hard to think straight.

"Yeah. I'm fine," I mumble.

I can tell from the look in Jonathan's eyes that he doesn't believe me. This time Jonathan stops dancing his focus on someone behind me. I don't even have to turn around to know who it is.

Daniel.

CHAPTER FIVE

O'REAGAN
AN CHLANN

DANIEL

I should be focused on the attacks on my business. Not worrying about the guy who's dancing with Lily. After she left my office, I watched her on the cameras. Saw him approach her and take her to the small dance floor in front of the bar.

Violence vibrates through my system as I leave and approach them. "Is he bothering you?" I ask her but keep staring at him.

"N-n-no," She stutters. He still hasn't removed his hands from her waist. I consider dragging him away from her.

"I'm sorry, who are you?" The guy has the nerve to ask.

I grin at him, but it's with venom. "I'm Daniel O'Reagan. Who are you?"

My name makes a quick register with his tiny brain, yet he still holds onto Lily.

I step closer. I don't dance, so I have no idea what I'm doing. I know we are being watched by every eye in the club, but right now, I just want his hands off my property.

"Jonathan. Lily's friend from college."

Lily steps away from Jonathan. "What do you want?" Her words are angry.

She's still the same girl but so different. I hate the power she has over me. How nothing else matters but her, especially now when I'm up shit creek. But I suppose I could use her reappearance in my life to my advantage.

"How is your brother?" A sore spot that makes her flinch.

"He's fine. Why?" Concern soon tightens her features. "Is he in trouble?" Worry continues to make a path across her brown gaze.

"I'm only asking after his well-being, Lily. But I have no idea if he's in trouble."

She shakes her head. "You never ask questions without a reason."

She's right. Jonathan is standing stiffly beside us. I want to tell him to go sit down and take the weight off his legs.

"I never recall you being so...." I want to say angry, closed. "Suspicious."

She snorts. "I have to get back to my friends."

"No." I won't let her walk away again.

"You can't speak to her like that." Jonathan half growls.

I grin at him again. "You think she's all innocent and fragile."

"Daniel." The plea from Lily has me tightening my jaw.

I've had enough of tolerating her playing nice. I reach for her arm and direct her to the front door.

"What are you doing?" She's alarmed and tries to pull out of my tight hold. I pass security and nod at them before glancing behind me at Jonathan, who's following. He protests behind us as he's stopped from following me outside, where I take Lily.

"What are you doing?" Lily barks and pulls out of my grasp while making an attempt to go back into the club.

"Is that your little boyfriend you're trying to get back to?" My words drip with anger that I'm struggling to contain.

Lily blinks rapidly. "What? He's my friend."

"I don't recall you being so handsy with friends." Of course, she wasn't. If anyone even looked at her, I'd make them pay. Everyone knew she was mine.

People enter the club, and as they pass, their interest in us is evident. I take Lily's arm again and pull her to the side of the building. I have a million questions to ask her, but I don't verbalize them. Instead, I want to know who this Jonathan guy is.

"What's Jonathan's last name?" I ask.

Lily tries to yank out of my hold, and I push her against the brick wall, boxing her in so she has nowhere to go.

"Why do you want to know?" She's breathing heavily. Her perfume floats and teases me. I release her arm and let my hand trail down to her side, resting on her hip bone. The heat of her flesh I feel through her navy trousers.

"I want to know who you are associating with."

"You don't have a say in who I hang out with." She attempts to sound angry, but her focus dances across my face before landing on my mouth. Her small pink tongue flicks out, licking across her lips.

I smirk and reach up, tilting her chin so she's looking into my eyes. "Don't I?"

Her brows drag together. "We aren't together, Daniel." Do I hear a loss in her words? She walked away from me, so why does she sound so lost?

"I got the memo years ago, Lily." I continue to smirk. "What? You think I pined after you." I let a laugh turn her cheeks red. "People leave. It's part of life." I release her chin.

She blinks, and her gaze darts to my chest, that she is eye level with. She seems so small yet so destructive to my system.

"I know you didn't pine after me." It's almost a whisper, but I hear her words.

"Did you pine for me?" I ask bitterly.

When she looks into my eyes, something shifts, and her sadness turns to anger. "Hardly."

Just what I need to hear.

Without a second thought, I dip my head. She inhales a sharp breath when she realizes what I'm going to do. I press my lips against hers; the moment our flesh connects, something in me unravels, and I feast on her sweet lips, that are plumper, but my brain remembers everything about her, and every kiss we shared is back at the forefront of my mind. I press harder, wanting more of her, and when her hands splay across my chest, I push myself tighter against her. Pinning her completely to the wall. I want to fuck her. I want to fuck that prick Jonathan out of her system. My lips crush her as I try to erase the image of him with his hands on her.

Lily whimpers with the force of my kiss. My cock strains against my trousers. Her hands push against my chest forcing me to break the kiss.

"I can't do this." She declares. She pushes me again. I could keep her pinned easily, but I give her a small window of space.

"Do what?" I ask.

"This." She points between us.

She thinks she can run again and leave me high and dry.

"This is two people thinking about fucking each other. It's just a fuck."

Her cheeks darken along with her eyes. "I'm not sleeping with you."

I laugh and take a step back. "We shall see."

She's flustered but still stays against the wall. I thought she would have run off.

"It won't happen, ever." She spits. I hear the lie in her words. "I don't want you near me."

Her words sting, but I place my hands in my pockets like they don't bother me.

"If you don't want me near you, then why are you still here?" I question.

It's the release she needs, and she pushes off the wall and runs back into the club.

She can run, but this time she won't get away from me.

CHAPTER SIX

O'REAGAN
AN CHLANN

LILY

I gather my jacket and bag. "Who is that guy?" Jonathan asks, flustered.

"He's hot." Crystal pipes in.

"And very fucking generous." Kieran knocks back his drink. I can smell the Red Bull, which is no doubt laced with Vodka.

"No one." I find myself mumbling.

Jonathan's green eyes plead with me.

"I'm tired. I'm going to call it a night."

Johnathan nods. "I'll come with you."

I shake my head before putting on my jacket. "I'm fine. Seriously, stay. Enjoy yourself."

Johnathan doesn't look happy, but I can't stay here for a second longer. The kiss that Daniel placed on my lips still burns. I find myself licking them.

Laura is watching me closely. "I'll text when I'm home." I fire over my shoulder. Outside, the air doesn't help my racing heart. I tighten my jacket around me and look around for a taxi; instead, I find a security man I spotted in the club approaching me.

"Mr. O'Reagan has instructed me to give you a lift home."

I snort and glance around, searching for the man in question. Mr. O'Reagan. It suits him. I knew he was made for something bigger than just dodgy deals.

"Tell Daniel I'm fine." I keep walking, and when the security man follows me, I stop and spin.

"He insists." He looks almost apologetic.

Like hell I was taking anything from him. He had grinned at me like I was nothing but some pining woman who would be delighted to jump into his bed. That kiss has my head jumbled. Sleeping with him would destroy me completely.

"I said no." I wave down a taxi, and before the security man can say anything more, I jump in and rattle off my address.

Once the car is in motion, I lean against the headrest and close my eyes. Everything about him was formidable. Everything about Daniel always was. That's why he got everyone to do his bidding. A look from him could either make you turn into a puddle at his feet or make you quiver in fear.

A shiver snakes around the base of my neck, and I open my eyes. He had asked about Eric, my baby brother.

I root my phone out of my purse and call him.

"What's up, sis?" Eric answers, and relief crashes into me. I sit up straighter in the taxi.

"Are you in trouble?" I ask.

I can hear the sounds of his PlayStation in the background. "Give me a second," he says to whomever he's with. The noise grows distant. "No, why, what's wrong?"

I glance out the window at the streetlights. Everything is wrong. Seeing Daniel, hearing him ask about my brother.

"Nothing. I just wanted to make sure you were okay. Are you still working?"

He snorts down the phone. "Yeah, but I'd rather ...."

I cut him off and sit even straighter in my seat. "You will keep that job, Eric. I gave them my word that you were reliable."

"Calm down, sis. Jesus, why are you always busting my balls? I haven't missed a day. Don't worry. Your perfect reputation is still intact."

I close my eyes briefly. He can be a little shit at times, but he's my baby brother, and I want to keep him as far away from our uncle as I can.

"Are you coming to Ma's for dinner tomorrow?" he asks.

"Yeah. I'll be there." Sunday roast with my mother is something I hate. But it's every Sunday, and it's a tradition.

"Get some sleep, and don't stay much longer on the PlayStation."

I hear the noise of the PlayStation returning. "Yeah, Ma."

His sarcasm isn't appreciated. Our mother wouldn't care if he never got a job. In fact, I think she would be proud of him if he fell in with the family business. I know my being an accountant isn't something she brags about.

"Love you," I say.

"Love you too," Eric mumbles before hanging up.

The taxi pulls up to my apartment complex on Boyne Road. I slip the driver a tenner and get back two euros in change. I slip from the taxi and walk across the dark parking lot. I have a horrible feeling of being watched and find myself glancing over my shoulder several times. I run the last few meters and feel foolish when I stand safely in the elevator that takes me to the fourth floor.

The key slides into my door, and I turn on the lights before bolting the door behind me.

I walk to the windows and draw the curtains. I can't shake off the feeling of being watched. I turn on every light as I move through my two-bed apartment. One room has a single bed and a treadmill. The other has a queen bed, and I love my own space away from my mother. I return to the main living room and click on the electric fire. The flames pop up behind the screen, and heat immediately emanates from it. The complex is fairly new, and each apartment is decorated with all the up-to-date modern conveniences. My favorite is my large American-style fridge. I open the door and take out a bottle of Prosecco. Taking down a wine glass, I fill it and take a deep gulp. As I glance around my living space, my body seems to slump.

Daniel O'Reagan. I thought I'd never see him again. I go through our interactions and linger longer than is normal on the kiss. I guess he kisses all the girls like that. Makes them melt at his feet. Since my mother and uncle shipped me to England to start a new life, I've barely had anything that resembled a normal relationship. How does anyone compare to him? I finish the glass of wine, but it doesn't settle my nerves. My stomach hasn't settled either. Butterflies are putting on the performance of their lives. I shake out of my jacket.

My phone dings, and my heart jumps. Fishing the phone out of my bag, I open the message from an unknown number.

This isn't over.

Three words that send my heart crashing and a spike of fear through my system.

It never was over, Daniel. Not for me, anyway. I'm staring at his message when a loud bang rattles my front door. I'm clutching the phone and staring at the door.

Did he follow me home? With a hammering heart, I walk to the door and hope against all hopes it isn't him. I don't think I could resist him if he was here in my home. I barely escaped his kiss.

CHAPTER SEVEN

O'REAGAN
AN CHLANN

DANIEL

After Lily leaves, so does her so-called friend Jonathan. She refused a lift from my driver. Her pride won't last long.

"Keep an eye on things. I have to step out for a while." I tell Franko, my right-hand man. Tonight is opening night, and I had no intentions of leaving, but I don't like the idea of Jonathan following Lily home when one of my security overheard her saying no to him already. I'd have to teach him a lesson.

My driver followed her home to an apartment complex on Boyne Road. My phone dings as I get into my car.

I have Jonathan. Should I hold him until you get here?

I stop at a set of traffic lights on Dublin Road. **Yes. I'll be there in five minutes.**

I put the phone down as the traffic starts to move again. The cars move in a steady line. There aren't many out at this hour of the night. When I pull up across the road from the complex, I spot my driver's car parked along a curb. I get out and lock my car before jogging across the road. I open the back door and slide in beside a frazzled Jonathan.

"This is kidnapping," he says the minute he sees me.

"You aren't a kid. And this is a warning. You stay away from Lily."

He glances at the dark-tinted window that divides the driver from us before his gaze shoots back to me. "I work with Lily. We are friends."

I grin. "That sounds like a no to me."

He swallows, and I want to throttle him, but I restrain myself for a moment. "This is how it's going to go. My driver will take you home, where you will lie in bed and think about my warning. Understanding that this could go two ways, the other doesn't end well for you."

His face turns red with anger, but he wisely keeps his mouth shut.

"Are we done here?" He asks.

I smirk. "For now." I get out and close the door before tapping on the roof. Walking to the footpath, the car pulls away with its cargo in tow. I hope he heeds my warning and leaves. I enter the apartment building and don't like how the access to Lily was so easy. The doors to most apartment complexes are normally locked, but someone has left it open. I close it behind me and glance at the long row of mailboxes. I search for Lily's name and find her. Thankfully, she had informed me she was using her mother's maiden name, or I wouldn't have been sure if it was her apartment.

Floor four, apartment number six. I take the elevator to the fourth floor, and I have an excitement buzzing in my blood at seeing Lily again. That kiss was only the start, and I always finish what I start. The doors slide open, and I enter an empty but well-kept long corridor. Overall I don't mind her staying here. I'm not happy about the front door being left open, something I will have to speak to the complex owner about. I don't like the thought that Lily could be accessed so easily.

I stop at her door and knock. It doesn't take long for her to open the door. Shock is visible in her widening gaze.

"What are you doing here?" She steps closer and glances out into the hallway. "How did you even know where I lived?"

I ignore her questions and have this eagerness to see her home, to learn everything I have missed about her.

"Are you not going to invite me in?" I ask.

She folds her arms over her chest. "If I say no...."

I tilt my head and pretend to ponder the idea of not being let in. I could walk right in, but I want to give her a moment to make the right choice.

She chews on her lip, and I wonder if she's thinking about our kiss. She finally drops her hands and steps back.

"I'm getting ready to go to bed, so whatever it is, make it quick."

I step into her apartment and glance around. "I don't do anything quick," I say, but I continue to inspect her home. The kitchen is a decent size, and the counters are clear of clutter. She was always spotless. A bottle and glass of wine, along with her coat, sit on the opposite counter. I walk into the living space. A small electric fire gives out a nice amount of heat, and I shrug out of my suit jacket and place it on the back of her couch.

"Don't get comfortable." She remarks while hesitantly closing the door.

I take a look at her. "You refused a lift from my driver." I state and take a step closer to her.

She runs her hands down the side of her trousers. "I can make my own way in life, Daniel. I don't need a driver." Is that a sneer I hear in her words?

"I would feel better if you took a lift from my driver." I remark, taking another step toward her.

"I don't care how you feel."

That much is true. If she cared about me even for a second, she wouldn't have run off to start her new life.

I grin like her words bounce off my silver armor. "You might not care how I feel, but you like how I make **you** feel." I stop right in front of her. Reaching out, I take her face in my hands. She doesn't fight me or push me away as I bring my lips to hers. I can taste the wine on her tongue as I suck the fleshy pink meat. She groans into my mouth, but after a moment, she pushes me away and moves across the room like that will help.

"I want you to leave." She points at the door.

That isn't going to happen.

"No."

CHAPTER EIGHT

O'REAGAN
AN CHLANN

LILY

My heart hammers in my chest. Daniel appears relaxed, like my telling him I don't care about his feelings or that I want him to leave, doesn't bother him. Maybe it doesn't. But it bothers me. Is that what he is here for, just sex? As I take in his wide shoulders, which are wider than I remember, my stomach dips. I remember how having him inside me felt. I tighten my legs together.

"I want you to leave."

He pushes a hand through his blond hair that's gotten longer; it suits him. "Why don't you say that again, but this time convince me?" His grin sends my heart racing.

"What do you want?" I ask again.

"I want to fuck you." He says it plainly. The smirk leaves his lips that I want to have pressed against mine so badly. So why not just do it as a goodbye that I never got to give him?

I can't believe I'm doing this; I think as I walk across the space. Surprise flashes in his gaze as I reach up and wrap an arm around his neck, dragging his mouth down to mine. His lips are warm, and he's quick to catch on. His arms wrap around my waist, dragging my body into his.

My fingers grow frantic as I try to open the buttons of his shirt with an earnestness I can't hide. After a bit of fiddling, I finally get to push the shirt down his shoulders. I want to see him. I break the kiss and take in his chiseled chest. I reach out and touch the three swallows that have been tattooed over his heart. This is new. He never had these before. My fingers drop lower to the scar that runs along his torso. It's vicious looking but not recent; it just hasn't healed very well.

When my gaze travels back to him, I want to ask what he endured while I was away, but his intentions are clear as he pulls me back into his chest and slams his mouth back onto mine.

I have often heard the phrase that a kiss can make your toes curl, but I've never really experienced it until this moment. It's like Daniel sucks the life out of me, and I slump against his chest, my toes curl in my shoes as my body buzzes. I'm airborne in a second as Daniel carries me to the bedroom. This close to his face, I spot a small white scar on his forehead. I brush back the blond hair that has fallen down onto his forehead, and my fingers dance along another new scar that wasn't there before. Once again, I have the urge to ask him what happened, but I find myself being laid down on the bed, and Daniel doesn't waste a moment before his body is pressed against mine, his lips devouring my mouth.

Large hands reach under my shirt, and his fingers tighten around my breasts. A gasp has my eyes springing open. Daniel is watching me, and the look in his eyes is deadly. The blood freezes in my veins, and the lust I had felt moments ago flees. I try to sit up, but his hands tighten around my breast.

"I'm going to fuck you." Why does he sound like he'd rather do anything else?

All of a sudden, I'm not sure about this. I try to rise again, but Daniel isn't moving. "Daniel?" I question as he glances down at me with an unreadable expression on his face.

"Where is your uncle?" His question expels any want or good thoughts I had about Daniel.

"That's why you are here." This time when I rise, he lets me. I stand and turn. Daniel still lies half across the bed in the same position.

"I need to find him, Lily."

"I don't know where Mike is." My stomach curls. That's why he is here. To find my uncle. I don't ask what he did. I don't want to know.

"Get out of my home," I say.

Daniel rises from the bed but sits on the edge before running his hands through his hair. "This isn't some fucking game, Lily."

"Get! Out! Of! My! Home!" Looking at him is setting every nerve ending on fire. I loved him, love him, and he's here to torture me again. I can't do this.

He rises like I didn't just roar the house down. "You are going to help me find him." As he buttons up his shirt, I want to punch him so badly, but I am not a violent person.When he finishes buttoning his shirt, he glances at me. "Because if you don't, I will do what your brother always wanted me to do and give him a job."

I clear the space and raise my hand to land a slap on his smug face. He catches my hand mid-air, fingers tightening around my wrist.

"That's not happening; you will leave my brother out of this."

He releases my wrist, and I rub the tender flesh.

"Of course I will. Once you help me find Mike."

My heart drums rapidly. I want to tell him I hate him. But if I did, this wouldn't hurt so much.

"I swear, Daniel, I don't know where he is."

"You are a resourceful girl; I'm sure you will find a way." He walks past me and out of my room. It takes me a moment to kick into gear, and I follow him into the living space. He shrugs into his suit jacket.

"I'll ask my mother tomorrow at Sunday dinner," I finally say. Knowing she will know where her brother is.

Daniel stops and glances at me. "See how resourceful you are."

I grit my teeth, refusing to answer.

"Does your mother still live in the same house?" he asks.

I'm tempted not to answer, but there is no point. "Yes, why?"

"I'll see you for dinner at your mother's tomorrow."

I'm shaking my head. "That's not happening."

He smirks. "I'm not asking your permission. See you tomorrow." Daniel stops at the door, and before leaving, he pauses. "That door downstairs needs to be kept closed. You never know who's around."

I snort. "Yeah, like you."

I can't see his face, and I don't know why, but I picture him grinning.

The door closes, and all I want to do is scream.

CHAPTER NINE

O'REAGAN
AN CHLANN

DANIEL

The two-story townhouse is pretty much the same as I remember it. I had spent many nights here with Lily; each memory is fresh and accompanied by a stab of pain that makes me more determined to get the information I seek.

I park on the quiet street. In the distance, I hear an electric lawn edger, but that's the only sound that greets me. My car beeps as I lock it and make my way to the front of the house. Sun reflects off the recently cleaned windows. That's one thing about Lily's mother; she kept a spotless home. She took great pride in her home. Every window is open, and as I raise my hand to knock on the door, I pause; it's been left ajar.

"Hello." I call as I step into the hallway. Not much has changed here, either. She still has the black and gray striped wallpaper. The flooring might be different, but I don't have time to inspect the space as Lily's mother smiles at me from the kitchen door. A snow-white apron is wrapped around her small waist. Cigarette smoke rises from in-between her fingers.

She holds out her free arm. "You might be big, but I can still get a hug." Her gaze stays on me as I walk to her. Sorcha may appear like a regular housewife, but I know how deeply she has fallen into a life of crime. I'm sure her house is used to stash weapons that have ended many lives. I'm sure she knows secrets that would be worth a lot to a man like me.

I step into her one-armed embrace. The smell of her favorite perfume, Charlie, engulfs me, and just like that, another wave of memories hits me, ones I had forgotten about. Mostly of being in this kitchen as we ate pancakes, and she watched us as she leaned against the counter, always with a lit cigarette in her hand and a smile on her face.

"Great to see you, Sorcha," I say, breaking the embrace. She waves the smoke away and walks into the kitchen.

"I was shocked when Lily said you would be joining us." Sorcha bends at the waist to look into the oven where a roast is cooking.

"I met her last night, and she insisted," I say as I sit down.

Sorcha straightens and wipes one hand on the front of her apron. She raises a brow, and I grin.

"Maybe I invited myself."

She purses her lips and nods her head. "That sounds more like it. Lily isn't exactly friendly." She stubs out the cigarette, and I suddenly want to learn more about Lily.

But speak of the devil, and he shall appear springs to mind as Lily calls from the front door.

"Hi, Mammy."

"Daniel is here, baby." Her mother calls while giving me a quick glance. I'm sure she's wondering how Lily will react to my appearance.

Lily enters the kitchen, and she is a wall of hostility and nerves. "Yeah, I know." Lily half growls.

Lily places her bag on the countertop before shrugging out of a navy cardigan. She's looking over her mother's shoulder. "It smells great," she says, and I use the moment to take her in as her mother offers her a teaspoon of gravy to taste.

The dark denim jeans are painted onto her long curvy legs. The cream sweater fits her snugly. Her dark brown hair is tied up in a high ponytail. With any other girl, they would look basic, but when Lily turns with fire in her eyes and some gravy on her lip, my cock tells me she isn't basic. Far fucking from it.

Her tongue flicks out and licks the gravy.

"Go, sit down. I'll start dishing out." Her mother ushers her away. Lily is hesitant but sits down just as the front door opens again.

Music blasts from Eric's ear pods that hang around his neck. He marches to his mother but pauses when he notices me at the table.

"Daniel." His smile is instant as he walks to me and holds out a hand. I get out of the chair and take his hand as he pulls me into a half hug. When we break away, I ruffle his hair like I used to. "You got big," I say.

He fixes his hair as I sit back down. "Well, you're a fucking giant."

"Mind your language," Sorcha says.

Eric sits beside me. "How has work been?"

He's too easy. I grin and tilt my head. I want to look at Lily to see her reaction, but instead, I lean into Eric. "Great."

He glances at Lily and shakes his head. "I'm working a deadbeat job."

"It's honest," Lily says with her head held high.

I sit back as Sorcha approaches the table and places a plate in front of me.

"No one got rich on honesty." She tells us all.

"Every criminal dies young, Mother." Lily bites out; her jaw clenched with anger. This must be a long-standing argument between them.

"I just opened a new club," I say, and all eyes fall on me.

Eric is nodding already; his eagerness should delight me, but instead, I hate how he can't see Lily is trying to protect him.

"I could give you a job."

"Fuck yeah." He grins at Lily.

"No," Lily says no straight away.

Sorcha places Lily's dinner in front of her before going to get Eric's.

" Language," Sorcha remarks as she places Eric's plate in front of him.

"It would be bar work, but there is room to climb the ranks."

Eric's smile dwindles. "Like pulling pints and shit?"

I nod before I start to cut into the tender beef.

The two-story townhouse is pretty much the same as I remember it. I had spent many nights here with Lily; each memory is fresh and accompanied by a stab of pain that makes me more determined to get the information I seek.

I park on the quiet street. In the distance, I hear an electric lawn edger, but that's the only sound that greets me. My car beeps as I lock it and make my way to the front of the house. Sun reflects off the recently cleaned windows. That's one thing about Lily's mother; she kept a spotless home. She took great pride in her home. Every window is open, and as I raise my hand to knock on the door, I pause; it's been left ajar.

"Hello." I call as I step into the hallway. Not much has changed here, either. She still has the black and gray striped wallpaper. The flooring might be different, but I don't have time to inspect the space as Lily's mother smiles at me from the kitchen door. A snow-white apron is wrapped around her small waist. Cigarette smoke rises from in-between her fingers.

She holds out her free arm. "You might be big, but I can still get a hug." Her gaze stays on me as I walk to her. Sorcha may appear like a regular housewife, but I know how deeply she has fallen into a life of crime. I'm sure her house is used to stash weapons that have ended many lives. I'm sure she knows secrets that would be worth a lot to a man like me.

I step into her one-armed embrace. The smell of her favorite perfume, Charlie, engulfs me, and just like that, another wave of memories hits me, ones I had forgotten about. Mostly of being in this kitchen as we ate pancakes, and she watched us as she leaned against the counter, always with a lit cigarette in her hand and a smile on her face.

"Great to see you, Sorcha," I say, breaking the embrace. She waves the smoke away and walks into the kitchen.

"I was shocked when Lily said you would be joining us." Sorcha bends at the waist to look into the oven where a roast is cooking.

"I met her last night, and she insisted," I say as I sit down.

Sorcha straightens and wipes one hand on the front of her apron. She raises a brow, and I grin.

"Maybe I invited myself."

She purses her lips and nods her head. "That sounds more like it. Lily isn't exactly friendly." She stubs out the cigarette, and I suddenly want to learn more about Lily.

But speak of the devil, and he shall appear springs to mind as Lily calls from the front door.

"Hi, Mammy."

"Daniel is here, baby." Her mother calls while giving me a quick glance. I'm sure she's wondering how Lily will react to my appearance.

Lily enters the kitchen, and she is a wall of hostility and nerves. "Yeah, I know." Lily half growls.

Lily places her bag on the countertop before shrugging out of a navy cardigan. She's looking over her mother's shoulder. "It smells great," she says, and I use the moment to take her in as her mother offers her a teaspoon of gravy to taste.

The dark denim jeans are painted onto her long curvy legs. The cream sweater fits her snugly. Her dark brown hair is tied up in a high ponytail. With any other girl, they would look basic, but when Lily turns with fire in her eyes and some gravy on her lip, my cock tells me she isn't basic. Far fucking from it.

Her tongue flicks out and licks the gravy.

"Go, sit down. I'll start dishing out." Her mother ushers her away. Lily is hesitant but sits down just as the front door opens again.

Music blasts from Eric's ear pods that hang around his neck. He marches to his mother but pauses when he notices me at the table.

"Daniel." His smile is instant as he walks to me and holds out a hand. I get out of the chair and take his hand as he pulls me into a half hug. When we break away, I ruffle his hair like I used to. "You got big," I say.

He fixes his hair as I sit back down. "Well, you're a fucking giant."

"Mind your language," Sorcha says.

Eric sits beside me. "How has work been?"

He's too easy. I grin and tilt my head. I want to look at Lily to see her reaction, but instead, I lean into Eric. "Great."

He glances at Lily and shakes his head. "I'm working a deadbeat job."

"It's honest," Lily says with her head held high.

I sit back as Sorcha approaches the table and places a plate in front of me.

"No one got rich on honesty." She tells us all.

"Every criminal dies young, Mother." Lily bites out; her jaw clenched with anger. This must be a long-standing argument between them.

"I just opened a new club," I say, and all eyes fall on me.

Eric is nodding already; his eagerness should delight me, but instead, I hate how he can't see Lily is trying to protect him.

"I could give you a job."

"Fuck yeah." He grins at Lily.

"No," Lily says no straight away.

Sorcha places Lily's dinner in front of her before going to get Eric's.

"Language," Sorcha remarks as she places Eric's plate in front of him.

"It would be bar work, but there is room to climb the ranks."

Eric's smile dwindles. "Like pulling pints and shit?"

I nod before I start to cut into the tender beef.

"It's honest," I state before looking up at Lily, who's watching me.

"I don't want him working for you, Daniel." She hasn't touched her dinner.

"Don't be rude," Sorcha warns her.

Lily shakes her head. "You leave my brother alone." Her words sound like a threat.

I grin. I want to ask her what will she do if I don't?

"Daniel is looking for Mike." Lily blurts out. "That's why he is here," she finishes.

That was fucking subtle.

"It's honest," I state before looking up at Lily, who's watching me.

"I don't want him working for you, Daniel." She hasn't touched her dinner.

"Don't be rude," Sorcha warns her.

Lily shakes her head. "You leave my brother alone." Her words sound like a threat.

I grin. I want to ask her what will she do if I don't?

"Daniel is looking for Mike." Lily blurts out. "That's why he is here," she finishes.

That was fucking subtle.

CHAPTER TEN

O'REAGAN
AN CHLANN

LILY

Everything about Daniel being in my mother's home feels wrong. It's wrong how she smiled sweetly at him when she was the one who sent me away. It's wrong how Eric looks up to Daniel like he's a god. It's wrong how my heart races each time he looks at me.

"I have some business to discuss with him." Daniel finally speaks after the crushing silence that followed my confession of why Daniel is in our home. Maybe I'm angry that he isn't here just to enjoy a family dinner, that it has to be something that benefits him.

"I haven't heard from him in ..." my mother pauses like she's trying to think. "Two weeks."

Daniel cuts into his vegetables and takes a bite. "Is that normal for him?"

My mother's fingers tighten on the cutlery. "Yes."

She is lying, I can tell by how the corner of her eyes tightens. My mother offers a smile. "If I hear from him, I'll let him know you are looking for him."

"So, about that job. Can't you give me something else, like being a driver?" Eric says, wanting the conversation back.

"No, Eric! It's not happening." I bark.

"You're not my fucking mother!" Eric storms out of the kitchen, and my mother gives me a look that tells me I've ruined Sunday roast.

What's new? I'm a constant disappointment.

"He's right. I'm not his mother. But, what choice do I have when you don't try to give him a better life?" I'd normally never air our dirty laundry in front of people, but Daniel is eating his dinner like nothing is happening. So if he wants to get on with his dinner, then I'll get on with this conversation.

My mother isn't fazed by my question and has returned to eating her own dinner. "A better life? Pumping gas is a better life?"

My stomach hollows. "It's better than him falling in with the wrong crowd and doing drugs."

"He's not a kid, Lily. Soon, he will make his own decisions. You or I won't stop him."

When I look up, Daniel is watching me. My cheeks heat up. I want him out of my mother's home. Out of my life.

"You got your answer; now leave." I know I'm pushing too hard. But I can't control the fire that's consuming me.

"Lily." My mother warns. She would defend everyone else but me.

I rise and walk to the counter, taking my bag and cardigan.

"Lily, get back here. Don't you dare walk out," my mother calls after me.

Normally that would be enough to make me stop and return to her, but Daniel has pushed me too far. I slam the door and walk down the driveway.

I walk past Daniel's Range Rover. A childish part of me wants to kick it, but I manage to stay composed and walk past the vehicle.

My stomach twists as I think of Eric. He's so eager for this life. Maybe I should stop standing in his way. I keep walking until the sidewalk ends, and I have to cross the road. I walk down a side road a short distance, which will take me across the railway tracks and toward my apartment complex. It's a shortcut that I take regularly.

A vehicle slows down, and I glance over my shoulder. Two reactions flood my senses, excitement that Daniel is following me and dread that he isn't happy about how I spoke to him at my mother's. He rolls down the window. "Get in." He hasn't stopped driving. I ignore him.

"Get in now, Lily, or I'll have Eric as my new drug mule." His words freeze the blood in my veins. I stop walking and glare at him.

He grins like this is a game.

He leans across, and the door pops open.

I don't know why, but I glance up and down the road, maybe looking for someone who could rescue me. But there is no one. I get in.

The lock snaps, and I glance at Daniel. He hasn't started to drive; the car idles as he stares at me. One arm is slung over the steering wheel.

"You have got to stop running from me." He leans closer. "I'm beginning to think you like being chased." His gaze dips to my lips.

I remain still, not daring to give in and lick my lips as my mouth demands.

"I want you to hear me out," Daniel says.

I fold my arms across my chest and don't speak.

"Your brother can work at the bar, pulling pints, doing honest work."

I'm already shaking my head.

Daniel's hand slips off the steering wheel. He unclips his belt and moves closer. The space gets swallowed up by his sheer size.

"I'm trying to give him an honest job. You know Eric. He is going to take one that will get him killed or hooked on something. I'm trying to help."

My heart hammers. I know he is right. But, even at Daniel's club, it gives him a glimpse into the wealth he could acquire. I don't want him to even have any exposure to that life.

"Your club is built on drug money. That's far from honest."

Daniel grins, but it's more like a snarl. "You didn't seem to mind that drug money when you were sucking my cock."

I'm so shocked at his words that my body reacts, and my hand races across the space, my aim is his face, but I'm not fast enough.

His hand encircles my wrist, stopping me. "Maybe you could suck it again."

I try to pull away, but his grip keeps me in place. When he laughs, my body reacts, and my core tightens. He brings my wrist to his mouth and places a kiss over my flickering pulse.

The kiss is tender, but the tight hold he has on my wrist causes pain to race down my arm.

"Your brother will work for me. I can either make him a runner or work behind the bar. The choice is yours." Daniel presses another kiss to my wrists before releasing me.

The lesser of two evils is to have Eric behind the bar, but the words don't want to leave my mouth.

And especially now, as Daniel clears the space, grips the back of my neck, and drags my mouth to his.

CHAPTER ELEVEN

O'REAGAN
AN CHLANN

LILY

His mouth roams over mine, and I know I shouldn't lean in and open my mouth, but my whole body remembers his kisses, remembers how feverish they made me, how greedy they made me, how complete they made me.

My heart pangs with that loss, but as his tongue slips into my mouth, my heart beats rapidly for an entirely different reason.

His hand has loosened on my neck, and I know I can pull away from him if I really want to. I don't. My tongue matches his tempo, and I'm moving back as he pushes forward. The crown of my head rests against the glass as Daniel has half climbed on top of me. I want to show some restraint. He was crude only seconds ago. My hands press against his solid chest, and instead of making him back off, it's like a doorway being opened to allow his hands to roam. My thigh burns as he drags his fingers up under the band of my top. His fingers touch my flesh, and I moan into his mouth at the contact. His touch permeates my system, and the rush shifts down my entire body, and pools along my feet before pouring back through me. It's too much; it's not enough. My fingers curl into fists, and I drag him closer.

His smile against my lips makes me stop. "I need an escort to an event tomorrow night."

His words trickle in slowly, and I'm looking into ice-blue eyes. His smell circles me before it feels like it attacks, and my stomach twists as the smell drives memories of us together.

"You're still wearing the same cologne," I say.

His jaw clenches his gaze bores into me. I have no idea what he's thinking, but my words have him getting off me and sitting in the driver's seat like we weren't just making out.

I straighten up and push away the sense of shame that accompanies his quick exit.

"You will come with me to the event." His hands clench the steering wheel.

"No." I wasn't going to be at his beck and call. "You asked to meet my mother so you could ask your questions. I did as you said. That's where this ends." I'm ready to climb out, my fingers tighten around the door handle, and I pull, but the door is still locked.

Unreal. Without facing him, I speak. "Could you please unlock my door?"

"You are going to realize very quickly, Lily, that I don't take no for an answer." His words are coated in anger.

This makes me pause, and I glance at Daniel. Since when was he this angry, this manipulative? Never. This is not the boy I remember. I see glimpses of him buried under a lot of anger.

"Well, I just said no, Daniel." My stomach squeezes, but I can't be weak like everyone else around him. I'm not a puppet. "Now open the door," I repeat.

Daniel grins, and my stomach plummets. "How is Jonathan?"

My mind races. I haven't heard from him. "Did you hurt him?" I ask, praying to God that he didn't. I mean, why would he? He wouldn't. Daniel doesn't answer, but his grin is no longer on display.

"He's a creep."

I'm shaking my head. "He's my friend, Daniel."

He snorts. "He was hanging outside your home the night you left my club. I caught him."

That doesn't sit right with me. I had told Jonathan that I wanted to be alone, yet he had followed me home, but what's even more disturbing is that Daniel followed him.

"Who comes to my apartment is none of your business." I know they are bold words under the circumstances, but once again, I feel the need to try my best and not let Daniel think he has any control of this situation.

"It **is** my business. You are my business."

His words elate me; they shouldn't. I try to squash the young girl fantasy of always loving Daniel and realize that we are not the same people we were.

"Your uncle torched one of my establishments, and you will help me find him."

So, I'm a means to an end. Haven't you always been, Lily? I sink into the seat, his words hurt so much, but at least he is being upfront and honest about why he's spending time with me.

"Did you hurt Jonathan?" I ask as if all the rest doesn't matter.

Daniel's jaw clenches. "I never laid a finger on him."

That didn't mean he didn't hurt him. "Did you order someone else to do it?" Guilt churns in my stomach. Could Jonathan be hurt because of me? I haven't heard from him.

"He's fine. He's lucky I didn't beat some sense into him hanging outside your apartment. There is something wrong with him."

Relief rushes through me that Jonathan is physically okay. That doesn't mean that Daniel didn't have words with Jonathan. There is no way he kept his mouth shut. I think Daniel would be incapable of that.

There are times I look at his charming, good looks, ice-blue eyes, blond hair, and he's like a model from the cover of some Gucci magazine, not an Irish criminal.

"I'll collect you at eight -thirty tomorrow evening," Daniel says.

Before I can respond, the locks are popped. I'm staring at the door.

"Wear something nice."

I spin and glare at him, but Daniel isn't grinning at me like I expected; instead, he's staring out the front window, his hands tight on the steering wheel.

I open the door and get out. I don't answer him, but already I know that I will be going. If I'm not ready at eight-thirty tomorrow, I'm sure he will come up to my apartment and make me regret disobeying him.

It's only a stupid function, I tell myself as I walk away from Daniel's SUV, which still hasn't moved. I take out my phone and send a text to Jonathan.

Are you okay?

CHAPTER TWELVE

O'REAGAN
AN CHLANN

DANIEL

I'm sitting outside Lily's apartment complex. It's eight-thirty, and there is still no sign of her. The SUV idles as we wait for her. For a moment, I entertain the idea of getting out and marching up to her apartment to find out what's taking her so long. There is another part of me that doesn't think she will come. Could I blame her? I blackmailed her into coming. I had two reasons; one was so that anyone associated with her uncle would see she is on my side and not his. Word would spread that his niece was on my arm at an O'Reagan event and send a clear warning to him to come out of hiding. He's always been protective of her. The second reason was for me personally, I wanted her with me. Every time I was around her, I wanted more.

A flash of red clears my thoughts. Through tinted windows, I watch Lily walk toward the SUV. She can't see me, but she knows it's my vehicle. The driver gets out and opens the back door for her. It's only then she sees me.

The red sequined dress hugs her curves perfectly. Her dark hair flows across one shoulder in soft curls. The light makeup enhances her stunning brown eyes, eyes that bore into mine. She's stunning. Her lips are held in a straight line as she climbs in, thanking the driver as she gathers up the tail end of her dress. The slit on her right leg opens as she gets in, but she quickly fixes the dress covering up all her honey-colored skin.

Legs that I remember being wrapped around me so many nights. I glance away as the driver gets back in, and we pull away from Lily's apartment. I take out my phone and make myself busy as my thoughts spiral with memories of Lily in my bed. Smiling up at me as our bodies lay tangled under the covers.

"Where is this event?" She shatters the silence with her soft question.

I don't look away from my phone. Call me a coward, but if I focus on her, I won't be able to stop the primal need to take every bit of her.

"Kells," I mumble.

"Will we be gone long?" She persists with her questions.

"I've got a room booked for us." My cock hardens at the thought of us sharing a room.

"I'm not staying in a room with you. I can get a taxi home."

My phone disappears as I look at Lily. She will constantly fight me every step of the way. Her eyes are narrowed, and she looks so fuckable.

"I have no idea what time the event will end; you will stay with me until the end." My words are sharp.

Her cheeks redden. "I'll stay to the end, Daniel, but I'm going home, then."

I don't agree or disagree. The rest of the drive, she remains quiet until we pull up outside one of my families' hotels.

The driver gets out and opens the door. I watch Lily's backside as she exits the vehicle; I'm right behind her.

My hand lands on the small of her back, and she stiffens for a moment before she slowly relaxes as we enter the hotel. A waitress with a tray of champagne is waiting by the main double doors that lead into the event venue. I take a glass and hand it to Lily.

"Thanks," she mumbles, taking it from me.

I take another glass for myself, and we walk through the double doors. The room is packed, and I sense Lily's hesitation, but as I continue walking, she keeps her steps beside me.

All gazes swing to us, the newcomers. For me, I know it's about who I am; for Lily, it's curious stares at who she is and what she is doing here. I've only ever attended these events by myself and never brought anyone with me, so I know tongues will wag.

That's exactly what I want to happen. I want everyone to talk about Lily being on my arm. But I also want to shield her from the stares. She seems to shift closer to me as the room settles around us. I nod at Shane and Shay, who nod in my direction. They are talking to some of the local politicians. That's what this event is, a way to keep them all close to us with an extravagant night.

"Just stay beside me," I say to Lily without glancing at her as we move toward a group of men. Darragh, my uncle and my father's twin brother who is nursing a pint like always, and beside him are Jack and Richard

O'Reagan. They are talking to each other. Darragh isn't engaged, he's watching me advance, and he forms a smile as I approach.

"Young Finn." He says with a smirk, his eyes dance with his recent fill of alcohol. I can sense Lily stiffens beside me. She never met my father, neither did I, but he was a topic I wouldn't be speaking about.

"Darragh." I nod at him in greeting as his gaze slides to Lily.

"This is Lily McGuinness."

Everyone goes silent. Jack and Richard really take Lily in, and I feel protective of her all of sudden.

Darragh holds out his hand. "Lily, lovely to meet you." Lily places her small hand in Darragh's and accepts the handshake.

"This is Jack, my cousin." I introduce him, and he glances from me to Lily.

"Nice to meet you, Lily." His tone is light.

I know Richard won't be as friendly.

"This is Richard, Jack's brother." He's the eldest and the most ruthless.

He grunts something before leaning into Jack and whispering. He departs just as quickly.

"He has someone he needs to talk to." Jack explains, and I watch Richard approach a wealthy couple. I have no idea who they are, but when Richard smiles and takes the lady's hand, I turn to Jack.

"He can be sociable when he wants to," I say. Jack and I are close in age, but we didn't grow up together like my other cousins. They are very close, I'm given only certain privileges because of who my father is, but I'm always looked on as an outsider.

Except for Darragh. I think when he sees me, he sees his brother. Maybe that's where the fondness comes from.

"Could I have a word?" Darragh asks. He wants me alone.

"I'll keep an eye on Lily," Jack says. I wouldn't leave her with any other man, but Jack is married and very loyal to Maeve, who doesn't seem to be here tonight.

When I look at Lily, she glances up at me. "I'll just be a moment." I place a kiss on her cheek, and she doesn't flinch like I expect her to before I walk away with Darragh.

"This better be good," I say.

CHAPTER THIRTEEN

O'REAGAN
AN CHLANN

LILY

I watch Daniel, and his resemblance to the O'Reagan's is uncanny. His uncle Darragh has taken him toward the bar. I'm left with Jack. I haven't been around him before, and his presence leaves me unsettled, but it's better than the other brother, Richard, who seems downright rude.

"We haven't met before," Jack says.

I bring the flute of champagne to my lips. "I've only returned home recently. I was studying accountancy in England." I take a drink, so I shut up. I have a tendency to babble when I'm nervous.

"How did you meet Daniel?" I can tell he's making idle chit chat as he glances around the room before his gaze settles on me again.

"We have known each other for years." I inform him.

The angry brother, Richard, makes a pathway back to us, and before he can say anything, I excuse myself saying I need to go to the bathroom. Jack gives me a nod, but I can sense their gazes on me, and when I look over my shoulder, it's not just the brothers who are watching me but also Daniel, too. My gaze clashes with his, and I quickly look away. My stomach twists every time he looks at me. I had made such an effort to look good for the event, and he hadn't said a thing. I tighten my fingers on the stem of my glass, feeling silly for even wanting a compliment from him. After this event, I had to put as much distance between myself and Daniel as possible. I'm tempted to take out my phone, but I refrain as I smile at people that pass by me. I don't know anyone.

"You look lost." I pause as a guy wearing a denim jacket smiles at me. His smile is kind, and I think that's the reason I exhale and relax slightly. He doesn't look dressed for the event, but he's the only other person who's approached me.

"I think I might be," I say with a nervous laugh.

"I didn't see you arrive. Which lucky guy are you with?"

His compliment makes my cheeks heat. I'm ready to say Daniel when I think better of it. "A friend."

His green eyes twinkle, and he runs a hand through his thick blond hair. "I'm glad to hear it. I'd offer to buy you a drink, but everything here is free. So maybe a refill."

I like his easy banter, but my glass is nearly full. "I'm fine."

He doesn't hold a drink himself. "Are you here with someone, also?" I ask.

He grins. “A friend,” he replies.

That makes me smile. “It seems our friends have abandoned us.”

“Your friend is very silly.” He leans in a little closer. I like that he’s talking to me, but I’m also not interested in that way.

“Mine isn’t.” He adds.

That makes me pause; what does that mean?

“Maybe we could skip this gig?” His forthcoming question has me glancing around, but Daniel is no longer at the bar. I have no idea where he is.

“No, thanks,” I answer, ready to end this conversation.

“Come one. You're alone; I’m alone. We could keep each other company.” When he leans closer, I smell the alcohol on his breath.

“No thanks, but nice meeting you.” I’m ready to walk away when his hand tightens on my wrist. His hand is rough, like that of someone who might work with their hands, not someone you would find at a place like this. I didn’t belong here, either, but now I’m wondering who he is here with.

“I said no.” I pull my arm back, but he doesn’t release it.

His smile is gone, and he tugs me closer. “I know you are one of the girls who works here, so don’t play hard to get, sweetheart.”

My stomach hollows out. “I don’t work here, so release me.” What the hell does he mean? That I am a waitress? But the way he says it makes me think of a whore. My skin crawls.

“Eddie, don’t you have work to do?”

Relief pours over me at Daniel’s voice. Eddie immediately releases me, and I want to rub my sore wrist.

“I was trying to get away from this one, but she wanted to see if I was on a break.”

My blood boils, and I open my mouth to defend myself, but Daniel laughs.

"Come now, Eddie. We all know that isn't true. Why don't you go to the restroom and freshen yourself up before your shift starts?" Daniel's voice holds no humor, and Eddie seems to be picking up what Daniel is saying and leaves. He makes a beeline for the restroom.

All the while, Daniel stands stiffly beside me, watching him leave.

"Did he touch you?" The question sounds innocent, but from Daniel's lips, nothing is innocent.

My gaze dances to my wrists, and when I glance up at Daniel, he's looking at my arm. He nods and finishes his drink.

"I need to use the restroom. I'll just be a minute." Placing his drink on the table, Daniel leaves and enters the same door Eddie had.

I swallow the remainder of my own drink, but something has me placing my empty glass beside Daniel's as I, too, make my way into the restroom.

My gut tells me Daniel is pissed.

CHAPTER FOURTEEN

O'REAGAN
AN CHLANN

DANIEL

"You shouldn't have touched what is mine," I say to Eddie. He's leaning over a urinal. Zipping up his jeans. He glances at me, and before he can react, my fist smashes into his jaw. He stumbles and falls sideways into another urinal before hitting the ground.

"I didn't touch anyone." He tries to get up but my foot lands on my chest.

"Wrong answer, Eddie." I remove my foot before stomping down into his stomach. He cries out, and the door opens; someone is ready to enter but takes one look at Eddie on the ground and scurries away.

I allow him to get up. “The girl in the red dress?”

Him referring to Lily, has my fist colliding with his jaw again. Blood spurts out of his mouth and lands on the sleeve of my white shirt. I stare at the blood. “Now look what you did.”

He pales while trying to nurse his face. “I’m sorry, Daniel. I didn’t know.”

I raise my fist again when the door opens. “Get out.” I shout over my shoulder without turning around.

“What are you doing?” Lily’s soft voice is filled with alarm.

“Ladies are next door, Lily,” I say while grabbing Eddie by the neck, so he stops looking at what is mine.

“Daniel.” She enters the bathroom. “Please.” She begs.

I release him. “You're lucky.” I warn Eddie.

He nods while blood dribbles from his mouth. “Get the fuck out of my sight before I change my mind.” He dashes past me and gives Lily a wide berth.

Her eyes are wide, her chest rises and falls, and she shakes her head. “Why did you do that?”

I walk to the sink and try to wash the blood off the sleeve of my shirt, but I already know the blood stain won’t come off.

“No one is to touch you,” I say while scrubbing.

“I never said he did.” Her words are choked.

I turn off the tap. I need to change my shirt.

“I can see the redness on your wrist, Lily.” My want to throttle him resumes, and I have a moment of considering finding him again.

“You have blood on your shirt,” Lily speaks softly.

“I need to change.” The door to the bathroom opens again, and the guy has the sense to leave.

"Come to the room while I change my shirt. I'm not leaving you alone again."

She swallows, she doesn't agree, but she also doesn't argue. I take that as a win.

I stop by reception and retrieve my card for my room. We are on the third floor, which is reserved for most of the O'Reagans and people of importance.

Lily doesn't speak on the ride up the elevator. When we enter the empty corridor, I keep taking quick peeks at her. "You look lovely," I say.

She stumbles, and her reaction gives me satisfaction. Reaching out, I steady her as we stop at room number 304.

She's staring at my hand on her arm; she won't meet my eye. When she drops her hand to her side, I open the room door and enter the suite.

The large drawing room table has been set with small pastries and sandwiches for us, for later.

Lily says she isn't staying after the event; right now, I don't want to go back to it.

"Are you hungry?" I ask her. She's huddled close to the door. "I don't bite." I tell her hoping she will relax.

"No, you do far worse than that." Her brows pinch together, and her hands run down the sides of her dress.

I walk toward her, and her shoulders stiffen. "I do, Lily. When someone touches what is mine, I will do far worse to them than what you just saw." I won't sugarcoat what I am. Who I am.

I reach out and touch her cheek. She surprises me when she closes her eyes and leans into my hand. "He got off lightly," I say while stroking her face.

My fingers dance across her cheekbones, and I stop when they rest under her chin.

"I'm not yours, Daniel," Lily says, her gaze flickers to my lips that rise into a smirk.

Not yet. That's the thought that drums through my head.

I step closer until I'm breathing down on her pouty mouth. She doesn't pull away from me as I lower my head and kiss her lips softly. My cock hardens instantly. No one has ever made my cock as hard as she does. I grip her chin and tilt her head, giving myself access to her warm mouth. She tastes of champagne and something sweet. My tongue sinks into her mouth, and she groans against my lips. Her pleasure has me reaching to the small of her back and pulling her into my raging cock. I'm picturing her mouth around it, her tongue running along the head. I let my hands trail all the way up and around her front, where I grip her breasts. She groans again, and I break the kiss trailing quick ones along her neck all the way down until I'm pressing my mouth to her cleavage.

"I can't, Daniel." She says the words with her eyes closed. I make my way back up to her neck before taking her mouth with mine again.

The ringing of my phone has me groaning. I'm sure someone has noticed my disappearance from the party. It's mandatory to attend.

I ignore the phone, but Lily doesn't. She breaks the kiss. "Your phone is ringing."

I exhale before getting it out of my pocket. I don't take my eyes off Lily as I answer the unknown number. "Hello," I say while pressing a kiss to Lily's neck.

"Daniel. It's Alexis."

"Who?" I ask. I don't recognize the female voice.

"I have information for you."

That has me stepping away from Lily, who's frowning.

"Information about?"

"Mike McGuiness." I hear the click of a lighter before she inhales deeply. "It's information you need now."

I turn my back on Lily as she continues to watch me. "Where are you?"

"I'm in the hotel where you are. Room number 24."

"Room number 24, give me five minutes," I say. That's the second floor. Alexis must be one of the working ladies for my uncle.

I hang up. "I have to be somewhere. I won't be long. Stay here and ...." I point at the table. "Have some food. Make yourself comfortable."

"Who was that woman?" Lily almost sounds jealous.

I stop at her shoulder and plant a kiss on her cheek. "Wouldn't you like to know?" I say before leaving her and making my way to Alexis.

CHAPTER FIFTEEN

O'REAGAN
AN CHLANN

DANIEL

I keep scratching at the blood splats on the sleeve of my shirt, but the stains aren't disappearing. I've destroyed enough shirts to know the blood won't come out. I stop what I'm doing and enter the elevator that will take me to the second floor. Taking out my phone, I send a message to one of my security to keep an eye on Lily. She might leave the room, and I want her kept in sight until I get back.

I pass three different men on this floor. Each one looked disheveled and distressed. They got what they paid for. I didn't have any dealings in this part of the business. I liked nightclubs and giving people their escape while on my premises in the form of alcohol or drugs. For me, that's where I draw the line.

The women that work here are willing, no one is forced, and they make decent money. Most of this is run by Darragh and Shane.

I stop at room twenty-four. I raise my hand to knock, but the door opens.

A lady with red bouncing curls and matching red lipstick opens the door.

"Alexis?" I quiz.

She nods and pulls the door open, allowing me in.

The room is shrouded in darkness – the bed neatly made. A scented pink rose candle burns on a nightstand.

I walk across the stained wooden floor and turn as Alexis closes the door.

She grabs both sides of her black silk nightgown that's been left hanging open unnecessarily. She's a very attractive woman, and if she gave me any indication that she wanted to fuck, I'd normally gladly do it, but right now, I'm glad when she tightens the belt on the dressing gown.

"Last night, I had Mike McGuiness in here with some friends." She starts and walks to the dressing table. She pauses, glances at me, and motions to the bed. "You can sit down."

I take a step toward her. "I'd rather stand."

Her lip rises along with one brow. "Okay." She opens a drawer and removes a pack of cigarettes and a lighter. She holds them up for me to see. "Do you mind?"

"Go ahead." I just wanted her to tell me the information she has so I could return to Lily.

She lights up her cigarette and deposits the box and lighter back in the drawer. "So, he's here with some friends bragging how he's getting his cock sucked on O'Reagan premises while he just burnt one of their fun houses to the ground."

The cheeky fucker. Not sure why he calls my nightclub a fun house; may be slang, or maybe he thinks I'm running a brothel from it. It didn't matter either way. He was a dead man. But the information Alexis is giving me isn't anything I don't already know.

Maybe she senses the impatience in me as she blows smoke into the air and continues talking. "He plans to burn another one tonight."

Now she has my attention. "Did he say where?"

Her features are tight. "He said here."

She continues to smoke as I think about all of this. I find myself sitting on her bed. She watches; each minute that passes has her pacing quicker.

"Should I warn the girls?"

I'm sure she already has, but it would make it official.

"How long was he here?" I ask.

Alexis' cigarette is smoked to the butt, and she quickly opens a second drawer while extracting a small blue ashtray that she crushes the cigarette in.

"Two hours. But he wasn't alone. There were three others with him."

"He was drunk?" I ask.

Alexis places the ashtray in the drawer and closes it before folding her arms across her chest. "Yes." She nods several times. "You saw him drink?"

She frowns as she thinks about my question. "Well, no. Drinks did arrive in the room, but ..." She tilts her head. "I never actually saw him drink."

My theory is that Mike McGuiness isn't a sloppy clown. So he would never come to someone's premises and tell their staff that he was going to burn it down. It's a distraction, maybe a message of how easy we were to infiltrate.

"You saw the other men drink?"

"Yes." She's sure of her answer.

"Gather all the girls who were entertaining them. I have some questions."

Alexis nods again. "I can do that."

What is Mike up to? It seems strange that the night my club is attacked, his niece shows up in my club. Maybe that is something I can use in this situation.

Alexis walks towards me, the belt of her nightgown open, the black and red lingerie underneath enhances all her curves.

"Since you're here..." She smiles up at me while running her hand down my chest.

"Maybe another time." I take her hands off my chest as a knock sounds at the door. I place a finger over my lip and step closer to her. "Are you expecting company?" I whisper.

She shakes her head. I reach for my gun, but I'm not packing. I'm being paranoid. She's a prostitute. Of course she would have men knocking on her door, but as I look through the peephole, surprise flitters through me. I glance back at Alexis, who's watching me. Her nightgown is parted, showing off her undergarments. As I grip the door handle, she doesn't attempt to cover herself up.

I open the door enough, so Lily can see Alexis.

"Lily, how can I help you?" I grin down at her.

CHAPTER SIXTEEN

O'REAGAN
AN CHLANN

LILY

I can't take my eyes off the woman behind Daniel. She's standing brazenly watching me, but I see the flash of irritation in her gaze at my disturbing them. I want to scream at her that he just kissed me before he came to her. My heart races, and when I look back at Daniel, I want to wipe that smirk off his face. All the time we were together, he never cheated on me; in fact, he never looked at any other girl.

This feels like a strange place to be. Daniel in a room with another woman. I kick myself mentally, reminding myself that we are not together.

"I just wanted to let you know I've rung a taxi. I'll leave you to it." I turn, but his hand reaches out and grips my wrist.

"We aren't done." His tone is deadly, and shame on me when flutters flow through my body and gather in my core. I don't want to be done with him.

Seeing him in a room with another woman has done something funny to me. I peek at her, and she's standing with her dressing gown open. Black suspenders with red frills cover her long slim legs. The matching bra barely holds her large cleavage. She raises a dark eyebrow when she notices me looking.

"I can do couples if you want, love."

My cheeks turn red at her comment. I swallow and pull my hand out of Daniel's. "No thanks." I know I should walk away but leaving him here with her is something I can't do. It's my turn to reach out and take his wrist. I tug and am surprised when he steps across the threshold and allows me to lead us back to the elevator.

"Is there something bothering you?" His question is said so sweetly. I'm sure the waves of anger are pouring off me.

I don't speak, and when the elevator doors open, I swear I hear him chuckle. I march back to our room and swipe the door with the card. The minute we are in, I want to demand he tells me who she is. But as the door closes, trapping me in the room with Daniel, I turn to him, and my anger sheds away. I lost him once, and I realize I'm not prepared to lose him twice. The realization hits me hard and fast. He's mine and no one else's. I've never given my heart to anyone else, and I don't think I ever could.

Rising on the tip of my toes, I press my lips to his. His hands remain at his side like he isn't sure. I want to make myself very clear.

"I want you," I say while looking into his eyes.

Something shifts; the humor that I saw there since I arrived at that woman's hotel room door evaporates, and his ice-blue eyes darken. His hand slips into my hair until his fingers tighten at the base of my neck. I'm waiting for him to say something, but instead, his lips crash down on mine. I'm moving backward until my legs hit the foot of the bed, and I'm slowly being lowered. Having Daniel's weight pressed against my body has me opening my legs slightly. My body recognizes him and responds almost automatically.

Gripping his shirt, I'm trying to pull him closer. His tongue dances along the edge of mine, and I moan into his mouth. He shifts above me, his erection pressing into my stomach. My eyes snap open, and he's watching me. Daniel breaks the kiss and stares down at me. He balances on one arm while the other hand cups my cheek. I'm drawn to the blood on the sleeve of his shirt. He had beaten that man for touching me; that has got to mean something.

"Take off your shirt," I say.

"You really want me." He grins while climbing off me so he can kneel and unbutton his shirt.

"I don't like looking at all the blood." I lie.

He must know I'm lying because his grin remains fixed on his handsome face.

I watch each button he pops, and I swear he's going slow deliberately. "I have clean shirts if you want me to put one on."

He is enjoying this far too much, but I can't look away from his ripped stomach. Each muscle is defined, and I want to touch all of his skin. He always kept himself trim and healthy, but I don't recall this amount of muscles. His six-pack takes up my attention, and as he crawls back to me, I swallow, but I'm not backing out of this.

"As much as I love you in that dress..." Daniel's fingers curl around the hem of my dress, and as he drags it up my thigh, the split widens. "I want it off you." He finishes pushing the dress above my hips. He bites his bottom lip as he stares at my black thong before his gaze drags across my chest and lands on my face. He leans in, and my hands wrap around his neck, wanting his lips on mine, but his mouth passes mine as he grips the zipper of my dress and drags it down my back.

"Raise your hands in the air." I do, and Daniel pulls the dress over my hand and deposits it on the ground. I pull up my leg to remove the high heels, and his hand covers mine.

"Leave them on. I think they are very sexy." He bends and presses a kiss to my knee before continuing to press quick small kisses up my inner thigh. "I remember exactly what you like." He presses a kiss so close to my core that my body hums, and I arch my back while lying back, remembering exactly how good he is with his hands and mouth. He always knows how to pleasure me.

His strong fingers pull my panties to the side, and I'm craving his touch.

CHAPTER SEVENTEEN

O'REAGAN
AN CHLANN

DANIEL

Lily's eyes are closed, her body arching toward my touch, and I want her at my mercy. I want her to have no way to escape. Climbing off her has her sitting up in alarm. It thrills me to see how much she wants me. Seeing her jealousy was new to me, and I will keep reliving that moment when she saw Alexis over and over again in my mind. It was fucking perfect.

"Don't move." I warn her and open the wardrobe door. This hotel room is reserved just for our family, and the wardrobe is always fully stocked with fresh suits and ties. It's the ties I want. I pull out four of them; the silk runs through my hands. I grab one more before turning to Lily.

She frowns, but her tongue flicks out and licks her lips in what I know is excitement. “Be a good girl and remove your bra.” I walk to the post of the bed and wait until Lily has her bra free. She lies down and raises an arm to me. I love the trust. I take her arm in my hand and press a kiss to her wrist before bringing her arm to the post of the bed. Using the tie, I secure her before moving to the other arm and repeating the process.

I climb on top of her and press a quick kiss to her mouth before I stretch out the next tie. “Lift your head.” This time Lily doesn’t obey, and I bend down until our noses are touching. “Do you want me to fuck you?”

Her breath brushes against my mouth, and I want her now, but I also want to enjoy this moment. I know I should be dealing with business matters, but after seeing the look of lust in Lily’s gaze, I couldn’t pass up this opportunity. She raises her neck, forcing me back, and I secure the tie over her eyes. She pulls her arms, but the restraints hold. I don’t touch her, but I take a minute to allow myself to appreciate how fucking perfect she is and how much I missed her body.

Her breasts are fuller, her nipples hard and ripe for sucking. My gaze trails lower to her abdomen, that’s flat all the way to the small scrap of material that’s covering her sweet pussy. I climb off her and grip either side of her panties. As I drag them down, she pulls on the restraints with excitement.

I bring the small black thong to my nose and inhale. Her pussy smells so sweet. I drop them on the ground and pick up a tie; wrapping it around her ankle, I tie her leg to the bed; once she’s secure, I run my fingers along the heel of her stiletto before I move to her other leg, this one I give far more room to move, but it still keeps her legs wide and her pussy on display. My cock bulges against my trousers; she’s fucking heaven sprawled out on display. She’s remained still, but from the rise of her chest, I know she’s listening, waiting, and sometimes the anticipation gives the moment so much more. I unbuckle my belt, intentionally making as much noise as possible, her head jerks in my direction, and I grin.

Her tongue flicks out, and she licks her lips as I push the trousers past my hips until they pool on the ground. I walk around to the side of the bed and peel off my boxers. My erection springs free, and I give it several strong strokes. The veins bulge along the sides, and the head of my cock looks ready to explode. I'm surprised my spunk isn't streaming from the head.

I kneel on the bed beside her head, and gripping her hair, I guide her mouth to my cock. Instantly, her tongue flicks, ripping a groan of agony and pleasure from me. I want to drive my cock into the back of her throat, but she's doing something with her tongue that's amazing. She runs it under the hood of the head of my cock, her tongue drags across the length of my shaft, and she returns to the head.

"Fuck." I hiss, it's so good.

Her lips wrap around my cock, and I can't hold back as I drive myself into her mouth. She takes most of my cock; she never holds back and always gives so much in the bedroom. My hands sink into her hair as I pound my cock into her mouth. She's gagging around my cock, and it drives me to move faster until I'm close to the edge, but I pull back, not wanting this to end. I extract my cock from her mouth, her saliva coats the shaft, and pre-cum glistens on the head of my cock. I run my finger across the pre-cum and smear it on her ruby-red lips. Her tongue instantly flicks out and tastes it. She sucks her bottom lip, and my cock jumps, already wanting to be back in her mouth. But, I want to prolong this as much as possible.

Walking back to the end of the bed, I position myself between her legs where I can enjoy the view while I play. She can't clamp them together with the restraints. I grip the lips of her pussy with my thumb and forefinger and roll. The effect is instant; she groans in pleasure, and when I increase the speed, she jerks against the ties on her wrists. With my other hand, I slip a finger inside her pussy and slowly press it to the roof of her pussy. The rhythm inside is slow as I roll her lips fast on the outside, her clit trapped between her folds.

She's groaning, and I remember how this was the way she loved to cum. I release her pussy, and her legs jerk like she can't believe I've stopped. I bury my head between her legs and suck on her clit. She's jerking and hissing under me, and I know I've hit the spot. While I suck, I dip two fingers inside her, and her wetness instantly coats my fingers. I don't want her to come like this. I want to bury myself inside her sweet pussy.

CHAPTER EIGHTEEN

O'REAGAN
AN CHLANN

LILY

Oh. My. God. I'm ready to combust. His mouth sucks my clit, sending all the sensations from my nerve endings zipping through my body. It's hard to hold still, and I'm jerking against the restraints until the silk material tightens on my limbs. I rub my head along the pillow, trying to remove the tie from my eyes. I want to see Daniel between my legs. I manage to uncover one eye when he looks up. He sits straight and wags a finger.

"That was very bold." My core tightens, and I focus on his cock that grows closer to my face, but he stops and refastens the material on my eyes. The darkness has me blinking behind the tie. My buttocks clench as his cock touches my lips; my body reacts so easily to his. I don't open my mouth this time. I want to taste his cock, but I also want to see him, and some deprived part of me wants to see what he will do.

"Open your mouth." My pussy flutters at his deep tone, but I keep my lips sealed. His cock slides across my lips, and I sense his fingers moving over the head; then his inhale of breath tells me he's jerking himself off.

I want him inside me. I finally open my mouth and let my tongue glide over his cock. His hand reaches for my head, and I know what he's going to do. I widen my mouth and brace as he slams his cock into my mouth and down my throat setting off my gag reflexes. I'm choking when he extracts his cock, saliva pools out of my mouth and down my chin, but I don't have a chance to think before he starts to fuck my mouth again. When I think I'm going to choke, he removes his cock, and he's gone.

I have a moment through my haze of lust to feel panicked. "Daniel." After a few seconds, I call out but relax when he climbs back up on the bed. His large hands roam down my inner thighs, and I arch my back, bringing my pussy closer to his hands, but he bypasses my pussy, and I'm not sure how much more I can take. He grips my hips, and like with my mouth, I know what he's going to do. Daniel was never gentle, but that's how I liked it. His cock fills me with no mercy, and it rips a cry from deep in my belly. He extracts before pushing back into me slower this time, and his cock fills me until it causes an ache in the base of my belly. He was always so big inside me and time hasn't changed that.

He pulls out and moves at a fast rhythm into me. When he pinches a nipple, the pain has me pulling my arms as I try to protect my breasts. My wrists burn as the restraints hold me back. Daniel pinches hard, and my core clenches around his cock that he's pounding into my pussy with all his strength. His movements are almost bruising. His hands leave my tits and clamp on my hips as he lifts my lower half off the bed to drive himself inside me. He's panting, groaning, and I know he's going to come before my back hits the bed, then he removes his cock from my pussy. Warm fluid splashes my hump and stomach, and I want to touch it, but once again, the restraints keep me in place.

My body wants release so badly. Daniel's cock covered in his cum reenters me, and I'm jerking my head while trying to tighten my thighs against him. He pushes into me slower this time. Fingers touch my lips, and I taste salt as he smears his cum on my mouth. The taste of him and his pace has my core tightening, and when he returns to playing with my nipples, I know I'm going to come. Every sense in my body screams his name. It's like my body knows he's responsible for this level of pleasure. I shatter across his cock, and a scream is released from my mouth that I don't expect.

I'm still panting long after coming, and Daniel still pumps inside me. "I've come," I say breathlessly, and he slowly stops and pulls out of me. My heartbeat pounds in my ears, and my body sags, molding itself into the mattress.

I've never felt so empty and in such a good way. A smile tugs at my lips.

"You enjoyed that." Daniel sounds proud of himself.

He was always amazing in bed, but after releasing all that pent-up want, my mind has returned to him being in another woman's room.

"Who was that woman?" I ask. The blindfold gives me courage for a moment until I remember I'm naked and tied up.

Material covers my body. "What's that?"

"My shirt," Daniel says, his voice growing distant. "You can just untie me." I call after him and jerk the restraints for emphasis.

I hear his footsteps, and the bed dips as he sits down. A warm washcloth touches my face, and for just a moment, I let Daniel take care of me. He moves onto my chest, and when he's done, he pulls his shirt back up over me.

"Untie."

"I think I like you like this. So, you asked about the woman?" I'm really listening, and I'm sure I hear joy in his tone.

"She was a prostitute." He answers.

It wasn't the answer I was expecting. "Can you please untie me?" I want to run from him.

"Are you jealous?" He asks.

"No, disgusted that you would lie with someone like that and then sleep with me."

He chuckles, and I've never wanted to hit someone so badly. I was an idiot for sleeping with him.

"I never said I slept with her." He's still laughing, but I don't find this amusing, not one little bit. Before I can say anything more, there is a commotion outside the room that has both of us pausing, and before I can react, I hear Daniel's footsteps walking away from me before the bedroom door slams.

"Daniel," I call as real fear chokes me. He can't leave me like this. I scream his name, but he doesn't return.

CHAPTER NINETEEN

O'REAGAN
AN CHLANN

LILY

"Daniel!" I scream his name again. How could he leave me like this? I'm yanking so hard that my wrists ache, but I manage to get one arm free. I reach up to pull the tie off my face when the door bursts open. I'm trying to scramble as men pour into the room, but the ties on my legs keep me in place.

"Gardai Siochana, ma'am, are you alone?" One of them moves into the bathroom as two more circles the room.

"Where is Daniel?" I ask. How could he leave me like this?

One of the Gardai approaches me and removes the blindfold completely. I wish they had left it on with the level of embarrassment that consumes me.

The Gardai is looking down at me, his gaze tracking my body that thank God, is covered with Daniel's white shirt. He narrows his gaze on the blood-splattered sleeves.

"Are you hurt, ma'am?" he asks, kneeling down to have a closer inspection.

"Could you untie me?" I can barely get the words out from the embarrassment, and the door has been left open so that anyone could look in. He immediately gets to work removing the ties from my arm and legs. I pull my legs closed and clutch the shirt tightly to my chest. One of the other Gardai, this one with a funny -looking mustache, hands me a robe. I take it with one hand, and with a lot of maneuvering, I manage to get it on and closed without dropping the white shirt.

"What is going on?" I ask when I think of all the commotion in the hallway.

"You were reported missing twenty-four hours ago. Your uncle claims that Daniel O'Reagan kidnapped you."

Shock roars through my body. "Kidnapping?" I ask.

The Gardai bends at the knees and places his hands on his thighs, and with a sympathetic look, he speaks low. "Did he rape you?"

What a fucking question. It's like a slap in the face. Daniel raping someone would never happen.

"We need to clear out the rooms now." A voice from the hall has the Gardai helping me to my feet.

"I need to get dressed."

He shakes his head. A pair of slippers appear at my feet, and I look at the young Gardai with the mustache. I can't process what's happening as I'm led from the room. I'm surrounded by Gardai. It's like they are trying to block me from all the curious gazes.

I'm escorted out of the building. Alarms blare from somewhere inside the building. I stop walking, and so does the circle of Gardai. "I need to find Daniel."

They look at each other. "We need to get you off the premises."

The shock and embarrassment are lifting, and I fold my arms across my chest. "I wasn't kidnapped. I want to know what's going on and why do I have to leave with you?" My heart thumps. I've always respected the law enforcement, but I can't just walk away without knowing what I'm walking into.

"There is a bomb threat on this building, and everyone is being evacuated."

"Oh, my God." I glance back at the hotel, and sure enough, now that I calm down, I see so many people pouring out of the venue. That's what all the commotion was outside the room. But, where the hell did Daniel go? Why did he leave me?

"Please, ma'am." The Gardai holds open the back door, and I climb into it. The minute the door closes, the sound grows distant.

The car dips as the Gardai gets in, and the engine comes to life. As I look back at the hotel, I hope there isn't a bomb, and if there is, that everyone gets out safely. I'm sure Daniel left with his high-profile family. I'm seething as I'm driven to the Gardai station. I feel exhausted.

"I don't know why I'm here. I already told you; no one kidnapped me. I have no idea why I was reported missing. I would appreciate it if you could take me home."

The Gardai turns off the engine. "We just have a few questions. It won't take long."

I could fight them, but they are just doing their job. I can't believe my uncle landed me into this.

I'm brought into a small interrogation room, and I'm left alone. I fight tears as humiliation has my throat and nose burning. I hope one day I can laugh at being caught by three Gardai strapped to a bed, but something tells me I won't because Daniel left me. He didn't even have the decency to return and untie me.

The door opens, and I'm surprised when a female officer enters. It's not often you see a woman in this profession.

She sits down, and she doesn't have the warmth I'm expecting. "I have a few questions, and then you will be transported to the hospital."

"Hospital?" I ask. This made no sense.

"You need to have an internal check." She says it like it's nothing.

"No one is touching me." I fold my arms tighter over my chest.

"A report was made that Daniel O'Reagan kidnapped you twenty-four hours ago. We received an anonymous tip that you were being held in room three-oh-four of the Headfort hotel in Kells." She rattles it off like it's nothing.

"I've already told your Gardai I wasn't kidnapped. I was there out of my own free will."

She nods and opens a file, and I see no one is listening to me. She pushes a photo across to me. "Do you recognize this woman?"

I glance down, and my heart stalls in my chest. I look back at the officer. "Why?"

"Answer the question, Ms. McGuiness."

She knows my name. “Yes, she was at the hotel.” The image is of the prostitute that Daniel was talking to.

“This lady here?” The officer taps the picture. “Are you sure?”

I study the picture, and with certainty, I nod. “Yes. I remember her.”

“Well, that changes everything.” Is all she says and rises with the file in hand.

What in God's name is going on?

CHAPTER TWENTY

O'REAGAN

AN CHLANN

DANIEL

When I left Lily in the room, I never expected to step into the hall and be faced with three guns pointing at me. Before I could react, I was taken to the floor and carted out of the building. It didn't matter how many times I told them I had to go back; they wouldn't listen.

"If you don't release me now. You will be sorry." I threaten, but I'm shoved into the back of a squad car with no explanation of what is happening.

"Suspect has been secured and is being transported to Kells Gardai station."

I jerk forward. "Let me the fuck out!"

One of the Gardai pivots in his seat. "Do you know how long you will get for kidnapping, rape, along with arson?"

I slam my shoulder against the cage of the Gardai car. All I can think about is Lily being tied to the bed. "Do you know what happens to gobshites like you?" I ask him.

He narrows his eyes before turning forward.

We arrive at the Kells Gardai Station, and they don't speak as I'm escorted inside. I want to tear them apart, but I try to push Lily to the back of my mind, so I can calm down and focus on the here and now.

I'm brought to an interrogation room, and only then the cuffs they placed on me are removed. With my hands free, I contemplate snapping the Gardai's neck. But the room has cameras. He's a very lucky fucking man.

"I want my lawyer," I say, tracing slow circles on the table with my index finger.

"Daniel O'Reagan, you are being charged with kidnapping, rape, and arson. Do you understand?"

I smirk at the Gardai. Normally I wouldn't bite, but this list of crimes is almost comical.

"Whom did I kidnap and rape, and what premise did I burn down?"

Another Gardai enters and sits down without a word. "Lily McGuinness was reported missing twenty-four hours ago when she was found she was tied up to a bed."

Normally shit like that would make me laugh.

"You better not have touched her," I say. My finger is no longer moving in a circle. I need to break something. I can imagine them finding her tied to the bed.

My gut twists.

"So you know who we are talking about?" The Gardai asks.

"Why don't you get off your lazy ass and get my lawyer." His jaw clenches, and I want to hit him square in the face.

He gathers the fake file and leaves me with Michael.

"What the fuck?" I ask straight away, trying to remain in my seat. The camera's are still on.

"Get me out of here now!"

Michael leans in and like a professional, remains calm. "They have Lily being interrogated in Navan. She has denied charges of kidnapping and rape. The only charge is arson, and they seem to have a witness."

"I want to be taken to Navan now."

Michael shakes his head. "I have one of my men there; they will keep watch over her."

My hand slams down on the table heavily. "I want to be transferred, now."

"I can't just transfer you, Daniel."

"What would it take?"

He shrugs. "I mean if you did something violent. We have no holding cells here."

My fist connects with his face. Blood pours like a slow trickle initially down his face before it runs faster. The room fills quickly, and I cover my hand as batons are brought down on my back and arms.

I'm dragged from the chair but feel victorious when Michael shouts. "Transport him now to Navan!"

The gardai who takes me to Navan is also on our payroll, and I sit up front as he informs me of what exactly has happened.

"Mike McGuiness reported his niece missing twenty-four hours ago."

George glances at me. "Normally, we would ignore such a report."

I wave him off, not caring for his explanation. I know why Mike was listened to. He's RA, and whoever took the call didn't want repercussions on their family. I don't like it, but I get it.

"Okay, so he accused me of kidnapping?" I ask.

"Yes. Said his niece would never go with you willingly, that she left Ireland a few years back just to get away from you."

That fucking stings because, most likely, it's the truth. I glance out the window, trying to hide the pain of that statement. "And the rape part?"

"She was found tied up." I can hear the accusation in George's voice.

I didn't owe him fucking anything. "It was consensual."

He focuses on the road, never commenting, and that pisses me off.

"You think I'm a rapist." I'm already questioning what I'm doing. George is on our payroll and doesn't mean shit to me, so why the fuck do I care so much?

"Of course not." He answers out of fear and not out of truth.

I run my hand along my face. "I've also been accused of arson. Care to explain that one?"

"We got an anonymous tip that gasoline used to burn your night club to the ground was in the back of one of your vehicles. It was searched today and found. We also had a witness."

"Who?" What a crock of shit.

"Some woman came forward; said she overheard you talking about an insurance job. She claimed you were drunk when you bragged about it."

The story sounds terribly familiar to Alexis'. She couldn't have double crossed me. She was too calm. There was nothing about her behavior that stood out.

"Did she have red hair?"

"Yes, I can show you a photo when we get to Navan."

She was a turncoat.

"Do you have a phone?" I ask.

George gives me a doubtful look. "I'll make sure you get your phone call when we reach the station."

I hold out my hand, sick of dealing with this juvenile gardai. "Phone"

He finally places it in my hand, and I dial Darragh's number. He answers on the sixth ring. "It's me; are you still in Kells?"

"Yeah, we got back into the hotel. They are doing their final sweep of the building."

"They won't find anything. Alexis caused this. She's working with Mike McGuiness."

I can hear traffic zoom past in the background. "Funny because I'm looking at her."

I take a peek at the Gardai, he might be on my payroll, but I have zero trust. "I'd have a word and get rid of the SIM card." I finally say, letting him know this line isn't clean.

"Thanks." He hangs up, and I delete the call from the log before popping out the SIM.

"What are you doing?" He asks as I roll down the window and through his phone out first. Then I bend the SIM so it can't be used and throw it further down the road.

"It will be replaced," I say.

"I had my family photos on that."

I glance at him, and I hope he can see the warning in my eyes to shut the fuck up.

He smartly does. Shortly after, we pull up at Navan Garda station. I would finally get to explain everything to Lily; only when I arrive at the front desk to be booked in, George is informed she isn't here.

CHAPTER TWENTY-ONE

O'REAGAN
AN CHLANN

LILY

I've been released, and to say I'm exhausted is an understatement. I have to stop at my mother's as I don't have my house keys; they are in my purse in Kells.

The moment I pull up in a squad car outside my house, my mother is out the door. The Gardai let me out of the back, and my mother wraps her arm around my shoulders, cutting the Gardai a narrowed-eye look before getting me into the house.

The minute the door is closed, she takes me in from head to toe. Her concern is something I haven't experienced before.

"Let's get you a cup of coffee." She stops at the kitchen table and places me in one of the chairs. I normally would never let her care for me, as I know it always costs something, but I'm too tired to fight, and right now, I do need some looking after me and some answers.

"Mike reported me missing," I say.

My mother's hand shakes, the coffee granules spill. She curses and starts to gather it up, wiping the coffee from the counter into her open palm. "Did he?" She questions, but something is off about her voice, just like I noticed the other day when Daniel was here.

"Yeah, he accused Daniel O'Reagan of kidnapping me." I watch her closely as she fills two cups with boiling water. "How ridiculous." Her answer doesn't make sense.

"I thought you would be horrified to think your brother was telling such lies. I mean, accusing someone of kidnapping is a serious crime."

My mother glances at me for the first time. "You're here, and you're safe. That's all that matters."

I shake my head, and she ignores me as she gets milk from the fridge.

"I don't understand any of this. Why would he report me missing?"

My mother returns to the table with the two cups of coffee. "I don't know."

"Does he hate Daniel that much?"

My mother tightens her hand around her mug, and it's the first time I see some regret in her eyes.

"Do you?" I ask.

She shakes her head. "No, I don't hate him at all, Lily." She slides my phone closer to me, but I don't pick it up.

"I was taken to the Gardai station and questioned. I was just dropped home in a gardai car." I want her to know the significance of what her brother did. I can't even tell her about being found tied up. My cheeks heat up.

"No one saw." My mother reaches across the table to pat my hand, but I extract it before she can make contact.

"I always thought you sent me away to England in hopes I would make a better life for myself. But when I came back, I was confused at how much you seemed to hate the life I was living."

My mother shakes her head. "I don't hate the life you have, Lily. I just want you to be happy."

I don't answer her. We have never spoken about how she shipped me off, and I had no choice. It was done so quickly. Mike had driven me to the Ferry and waited until the ship had left port. It was like he couldn't take a chance that I would get back off.

My stomach twists. "Was I sent away because of Daniel?" I'm whispering because I'm afraid of the answer, but I need to know.

My mother shakes her head. "We wanted a better life for you."

"We? As in, you and Mike?"

My mother won't meet my gaze, and that frustrates me. "Does Mike want a better life for me now? Is that why he's reporting that I was kidnapped?" My anger continues to heighten. "He's sick. I want nothing to do with him."

My mother rises. "Lily, he has your best interests at heart." She gathers up the mugs that neither of us have touched and takes them to the sink.

"I wish you would be honest with me. I know you know more. What aren't you telling me? A normal person does not report someone missing for no reason. Is Daniel a danger?" It's a stupid question. Considering the line of work Daniel is in, I know he would never hurt me.

"Okay." My mother turns with the dishcloth in her hand. "We sent you to England to keep you away from Daniel. It was for your own good."

My stomach hollows out. "You took me from the one good thing I had." I swallow the saliva. "What has Daniel ever done to you?"

My mother picks up her cigarettes and lighter. "Nothing. It's not what he has done; it's who he is." She lights her cigarette.

"You mean an O'Reagan?"

My mother turns to me and nods, blowing smoke from the corner of her mouth. "It's complicated."

"It still doesn't make sense to me. So he's an O'Reagan, what does that even mean?"

The doorbell rings, and my mother's gaze shifts to the front door, her gaze tightening. I have no idea what's going on, but she's nervous.

The doorbell rings again. "Are you not going to get that?" I ask.

My mother turns on the tap and puts out her cigarette, leaving the stub on the sink counter before going to the door as whoever is there continues to ring the bell.

They sent me away to keep me from Daniel. All these years abroad were just to keep a divide between me and the boy I loved. I never stopped loving him.

Pain and regret come hard and fast but are washed away as my mother re-enters the kitchen with Daniel, who looks worse for wear. I'm ready to ask him how he is, but I'm reliving being left tied to the bed.

In a few strides, he's beside me and squats down by my legs. "I got arrested for kidnapping and couldn't come back to the room." He's letting me know why he left me.

"I'm so sorry." I blurt, thinking about how much my mother and uncle have done. Shame burns my cheeks.

"I don't know what's wrong with him."

I'm pulled into Daniel's arms, and the whole day's events cause me to crash, and I'm crying into his neck. I'm crying for the years we lost together. I'm crying because of the unfairness of this situation. I'm crying because he's all I've ever wanted, and yet my mother and uncle keep tearing us apart. "I told them you didn't kidnap me." I mumble.

His hold on me tightens. "I know." He presses a kiss to my cheek, and when I settle down, he leans out and holds my face. "I'm going to fix this." His smile makes my heart jump, and I believe him.

CHAPTER TWENTY-TWO

O'REAGAN
AN CHLANN

DANIEL

I wasn't leaving this home without answers. Things were slowly piecing together. For me, I had thought that Lily and her uncle's reappearance in my life was a coincidence; it was calculated.

I get to my feet and look at Sorcha. "I think it's about time you started being honest."

She folds her arms across her chest, and I hate doing this in front of Lily, but I can't keep chasing my tail with this situation.

"I know Mike is RA." I tick that off my finger. "I know he seems to have it in for me since he attacked my club in Athboy. He also paid one of the staff in Kells to claim that they witnessed me burning down my own club." I take a step toward Sorcha. "I'm being accused of kidnapping your daughter and arson, all because Mike, for some reason, doesn't like me."

She still won't speak, but I can see the look in her eyes. It's one of regret and fear. Good.

"The night Lily came into my club was the same night my club was burned down. Your daughter is my witness; only now that I have been accused of kidnapping her, that alibi goes up in flames along with my business."

"Mike is RA?" Lily says in a small voice. When I glance at her, I can see she really didn't know. He's not high ranking, but he has always been associated with them.

"Yes," I answer, and Sorcha finally nods.

"He was only trying to protect her." She finally caves.

"From me?" I jab my chest. I would give my life for her. I'm shaking my head.

"From your association, Daniel. Your family screwed over the RA. He was afraid that if you two got serious, she would become a target."

"That's why you sent me away?" Lily is standing and walks toward her mother. "That's why you sent me to England? That's why I could never come home?!" The pain in her voice has me realizing that she hadn't just packed her bag and decided she needed a fucking adventure, that she was sent away, and it hurt her as much as it hurt me.

I should have done more to find her, but I had thought she wanted a new start away from me. Deep down, I had thought she deserved so much better than me, so I let her go.

"Yes," Sorcha says and reaches back, grabbing a pack of cigarettes and a lighter.

"I fucking hate him. Why has he had any say in my life?" I've never seen Lily snap, and to hear her curse startles not just me but also her mother.

"Don't say that. He does everything because he loves you."

"I'm going to the Gardai. I'm going to tell them he's RA." Lily erupts.

Sorcha pales, but I already know I won't let that happen. She's angry and lashing out, and that knowledge would only hurt her, not him.

"There is no point," I say.

Lily looks at me, and I hate the devastation I see in her eyes. "Yes, there is. He might stop interfering in my life." I take a step toward her. "They already know."

Her lip wobbles, and I see so many unspoken words floating around in her pain. "I should have come after you," I say.

Her lips drag down, and she blinks, tears spilling. "I let you go, telling myself you had enough of me and you deserved better." I admit.

She hiccups on a sob while shaking her head. "I never stopped loving you." Her confession makes every damaged part of me soar while trying to piece itself back together.

"Mike isn't your uncle." Sorcha speaks, smashing our moment.

Lily wipes her eyes as if she's just remembering her mother is standing there.

"He's your father." Sorcha admits.

Fuck.

I can see the impact of that knowledge coming down heavily on Lily. "My father?" She takes a step back, and I reach for her as she stumbles.

"He just wanted to protect you."

"Mike is my father?" Lily repeats.

Sorcha nods. "Yes, baby." She walks to Lily, and I release Lily's arm but still stay right beside her. "His association with the RA made you a target, and we couldn't have that. So, the safest plan was to have him act as your uncle.

"My entire life?" All the color has drained from Lily's face.

"I know it's a lot. But, it makes you less of a target." Sorcha reaches up and touches Lily's face. "It was done with love. And we couldn't allow you to get tied up with Daniel. It's too dangerous."

"I would have protected her," I say, and Sorcha finally looks at me, releasing her daughter's face. "I know that now. I'm sorry."

"Where is Mike now?" I ask.

Sorcha steps back. "I don't know."

"He burned down my club, Sorcha, and pinned it on me. You don't think he's gone too far this time?"

Sorcha chews on her lip. "He just wants you away from Lily."

Lily's sharp intake startles me. "You knew he was burning down Daniel's club just to keep him away." Before she can answer, Lily takes a step toward her mother. "You don't think explaining to me that Daniel is part of a rival gang and being with him is going to put me in danger would be wiser?"

"Would you have left him if we told you?" Sorcha asks.

I'm looking at Lily, and her eyelids lower. "I love him." She tells her mother, and her answer is clearly no. She wouldn't have left me.

My heart swells again.

"I need to speak to Mike to put an end to this, Sorcha, before someone does get hurt," I say.

She looks from her daughter to me. "He's here in Navan."

Lily nods. "Let me get dressed, and then we will go and speak with him. I swear I'll make him stop." Lily promises. I smile and nod at her. "Okay."

She leaves the room, and once she is out of ear shot, I drop the smile. "Where is he?"

"Daniel. He's my husband."

I nod. "You want Lily to come with me? You want her to see how ugly this can get."

Her lips form a thin line. "He's gone to Club Forty-Seven."

My club. I turn to end this for once and for all.

"Don't kill him," Sorcha calls after me. "Lily will never forgive you." She shouts. "And don't you die." I'm out the door and in the car when Lily, half-dressed, bursts out the front door. The look of betrayal on her face that I would leave should make me stop, but it doesn't. I floor the car and pull away with a promise that this ends today.

CHAPTER TWENTY-THREE

O'REAGAN
AN CHLANN

DANIEL

I arrive at my club on Ardboyne Road. It's busy at this hour, and the club is starting to fill up. I pull up close to the door and approach the bouncers at the door. "I want the footage of everyone who has come and gone here tonight," I say and walk past them, not waiting for an answer. Inside the club, there are groups of people drinking; some have already taken to the dance floor. I scan the crowd, but I don't see Mike anywhere.

I stop by the bar staff. "Any problems today?" I ask.

"No, boss, all is smooth sailing." I nod, but it gives me no comfort. He's going to attack. All of this to keep me away from Lily. I know my Uncle

Connor had ties to the RA, just like Shay. I knew there was bad blood, but I didn't think it would trickle down to someone like me. But, that is, if Lily were an average girl, she isn't. With her dad's connection to the RA, I can see how, if things ever got rocky, that she would be a target to hurt me or hurt him. But, Mike has got to know that no matter what, anyone who is associated with him is a threat.

Making everyone believe that Lily was his niece and not his daughter gave her a small layer of protection.

I enter my office and take out a fresh suit from the closet. The t-shirt I had grabbed back in the hotel room felt odd on me. I spent most of my time in suits. When I'm dressed, I sit down at my desk to open my laptop. The email with all the footage is waiting for me from the security room.

I have no idea what time to check, but I start when no one is here because that's when I would arrive. Delivery trucks come, staff slowly trickle in, and kegs are changed. Everything seems normal. I keep going until a fresh wave of staff arrives for bar work and security. Once again, nothing is unusual. I keep going until people start arriving. I'm moving the camera at double speed, scanning each male for Mike's face. A knock at my door has me pausing. Before I can tell whoever it is to enter, Darragh walks in.

"I knew I'd find you here."

"Well, what did Alexis have to say for herself?" I ask.

"She didn't say anything. I was pulled by the Gardai, and when I looked up she was gone."

"The bomb scare at the hotel was for the Gardai to arrive there and find Lily. It was a tactic to mess up our meeting with people."

Darragh slumps down in the chair across from me. "Well, he achieved that. I'm sure we lost trust with some of them. We can't even keep them safe in one of our own buildings."

I have a terrible sense of responsibility as this is because of me. "Mike doesn't want me with Lily. That's why he burned down my business in Athboy, and according to Sorcha, he was coming here."

"Who's Sorcha?"

I often forget that they don't know my past. I didn't meet most of my family until a few years ago after my father's death.

"Lily's mother." I don't mention Mike being Lily's father. It's already complicated enough. Darragh knowing that Mike just doesn't want me with Lily is enough.

"Shane is going to do some damage to Alexis. She's worked for us a long time."

I nod. "Her betrayal will be a reminder to the other girls not to turn on us." Everyone has to be made an example of.

"So, what are you doing?" Darragh jerks his chin toward the laptop.

I return my attention to the monitor and hit play. "Looking for Mike." I don't see him. The time stamp shows one hour before now, and still nothing. I'm shaking my head.

"He isn't here." Sorcha could have lied to me.

"You think Lily's mother lied to you?" Darragh voices what I'm thinking.

I pause the video and stare at the red-headed woman who passes through the doors. I sit up straighter. "Alexis is here." He's sent her. I follow her into the club all the way to the ladies' room; only she never comes out.

"Alexis went into the ladies' room and didn't come out," I say as I retrieve a gun from the drawer. I check to make sure it's loaded. Darragh stands and checks his own gun.

Excitement flashes in his blue eyes. "Let's do this."

I can't hide my grin as we both put our guns away and leave my office. I stop by security. "Empty the club," I say, and when I reach the ladies' toilet, I push open the door. Two ladies preening in the mirror startle. I hold a finger on my lips and motion for them to walk toward me.

They do, and no one else comes out of the toilets, so Darragh and I enter. All but two stall doors are open. I slowly remove my gun, and Darragh does the same. I nod at the door, and he grins again before stepping forward. His foot connects with the middle of the door, and straight away, it gives way and opens.

Alexis screams inside, and the phone she was holding falls to the ground. I point the gun at her to shut the fuck up as I pick the phone off the ground. The call is still connected, and I bring the phone to my ear.

"Hello, Mike."

"Daniel." He responds.

"I didn't take a member of the RA for a coward." I taunt.

He laughs, but the anger is evident in how sharp his laughter is.

Alexis shifts, and I move closer to her head. "I will pull this fucking trigger," I warn her.

She goes rigid.

"All of this because of Lily," I say.

He doesn't answer. "I get that you want to protect her. I mean, we all want to protect our kids."

I smile when he curses.

"I mean, I could use Lily against you, Mike, and now I have Alexis also." I tilt my head. "I don't think it was money that made her turn against us. I think it was more." I smile at Alexis. "Am I right? Do you love him?"

She glances away, but the answer is there in her eyes. "She will die because of you," I say and hang up.

Alexis starts to cry, and I have no interest in listening to her, so I step out of the stall.

"Should I finish her?" Darragh asks.

"Not yet." He will come for her. I know he will, but first, I need to know what she's doing here.

CHAPTER TWENTY-FOUR

O'REAGAN
AN CHLANN

DANIEL

"So what were you planning?" I ask Alexis. She turns her head away from me. Darragh kicks in the second stall door, and I keep my gun on Alexis while looking into the empty stall. Darragh puts his gun away and checks behind the toilet. He extracts something; it takes a bit of maneuvering to remove the device from the back of the toilet.

"A bomb?" I ask Darragh.

He holds the timer in his hands and nods. "Twenty minutes left on it."

When I glare at Alexis, fear tightens her eyes. "What do you think we should do?" I ask Darragh.

He steps up beside me with the bomb in his hand like it's a box of cigarettes. Even Alexis watches him nervously.

"I think we will strap this to her and send a picture to lover boy Mike. He will have twenty minutes to get here and defuse it."

Alexis starts shaking her head viciously. "Please, he won't come. He will let me die."

"I'm willing to test that theory. Now get up."

Alexis stands on wobbly legs. I keep the gun pointed at the back of her head as I take her out back into the delivery area. Beyond that are fields. I hope if the bomb goes off, we will be far enough away from the blast. Alexis is awkward climbing the fence in her red dress and high heels, but she should have thought of that before double-crossing us.

An old water trough sits in the middle of the field. Darragh joins us with duct tape and the bomb. He's whistling as he secures the bomb to her chest and runs the duct tape through a bar in the trough. Before he covers the bomb completely, I take a picture of it and send it to Mike along with a message.

Fifteen minutes and she goes boom!

Tears stream down her face as we walk away. Her muffled screams don't stop us. "So if the motherfucker doesn't show, what then?"

I shrug. I'm not sure. But, he's gunning for me.

"I heard you say that Mike is Lily's father. Why not use her as bait?" I stop walking.

"Don't ever mention her again." I'm toe to toe with my uncle. He outranks me ten times over, but I won't have anything like that said about Lily.

He grins. "Calm down. It was just a suggestion."

I glance at the phone. Twelve minutes left. I can assume he is close by since Sorcha knew he had come to my club. He must have been in the vicinity.

I stand at the fence line with Darragh. "When does this shit stop?" I ask him.

He lights up a cigarette. "Never."

I glance at him, and he grins. "That's what makes this so much fucking fun."

I snort a laugh at his passion for our lifestyle.

I glance at the phone again. Still nothing. We wait another five minutes when my own phone rings.

"We have someone approaching the club." My security informs me.

"Let them in." I hang up and nod at Darragh.

"He's arrived."

My phone rings again; it's my security. I see movement along the windows of the hallway that leads out to us. Darragh extracts his gun. I do the same as I answer the phone.

"Sorry, sir, we couldn't stop her." At that, Lily bursts out into the courtyard, fire in her eyes and determination in her steps.

"You left without me."

Darragh puts his phone away, and all the security pause at the door. I wave them off as I slide my gun back into the band of my trousers.

"It's not safe for you to be here, Lily." I walk toward her, trying to block her view of Alexis. But I can see by the shift in her shoulders, the large intake of breath, and the horror in her eyes that she spots her.

"Is that someone tied in the middle of the field?"

I reach her, but she shrugs me off.

"She was planting a bomb here. For your father."

She keeps staring at Alexis, and I need her to leave.

"This is wrong." She blinks, and tears fall. "You can't kill her."

My jaw clenches. "Lily..."

She zooms past me, and I don't expect her to be so fast as she sprints across the field.

"Lily, stop!" Real fear has me tearing after her.

"Fuck!" Darragh curses behind me.

Lily throws herself across a crying Alexis, who's screaming behind the muffled duct tape.

I grab Lily's arm. "Get up." I have no idea how much time is left, and ask Darragh.

"Four minutes," Darragh warns. We are too close for comfort, but Lily isn't letting Alexis go.

"Lily, you will die with her if you don't get up." What the fuck is she doing?

"Take the bomb off her, and I'll come."

I'm shaking my head. "We don't have time." I pull Lily again, this time with more force, and get her away from Alexis.

"You do this, and we are done!"

She's screaming.

"Two minutes," Darragh warns.

"I'm begging you, Daniel." Lily's pleas for me to let Alexis live shouldn't rattle me to the core, but if I do this, I lose her.

I nod at Darragh to cut it off. He hesitates.

"Are you sure? Because if she lives, Mike will know we are no good for our word." Darragh is right.

"Please!" Lily begs.

"Do it," I say to Darragh.

He kneels and removes a penknife from his ankle strap. As he saws through the duct tape, I notice movement coming from the field beyond.

Mike. He came.

"He sure cut it tight," I say.

Darragh has the bomb removed. "Everyone needs to run."

I grip Lily's shoulders. "You go with Darragh."

She sees her father, but she nods, and I'm surprised when she helps Alexis to her feet, and they all run back toward the hotel.

I, on the other hand, extract my gun and start running toward Mike, who pauses. He's spotted everyone running and does the same.

The explosion happens sooner than I expect, and the impact knocks me to the ground. The world tilts, and my ears ring. I roll onto my back, trying to catch my breath. The gun is a few feet away. I try to shake the sound in my head, but my ears ring as I reach for my gun.

A heavy boot clamps down on my wrist; the pressure is crushing, and I slowly look up at Mike, who holds a gun pointed to my head.

This is not how I saw this ending. His mouth moves, but I can't hear him speak. When he cocks the gun, I see nothing but glee in his gaze that he is going to end me.

He turns away from me like something behind him is distracting. With my free hand, I curl it into a fist, and with all my strength, I slam it into his leg. He wobbles as I roll but empties three bullets into the ground where my head just was mere seconds ago.

His foot becomes heavy, and I scream. "This time, you die." He says, and I'm looking at the gun.

Warm flecks of blood rain down on me. The weight is lifted off my wrists as Mike's dead body tumbles to the ground and right on top of me. He's ripped from me a second later, and I'm looking at Darragh.

"Are you okay?" He's pale, checking my chest and face.

I'm nodding. "Where is Lily?"

Darragh jerks his chin over his shoulder before helping me to stand. Sound pours back in; my ears ring.

It's then I see Lily lowering a gun. She's staring at her father's dead body, her eyes wide with horror. When she notices me looking at her, she starts to cry.

"He was going to kill you."

I clear the space and remove the gun from her hands. Alexis stands still, staring at Mike's body. "She got my gun," Darragh explains, holding out his hand for his weapon. I wouldn't imagine he did too much to stop her.

"I'm going to prison." Lily sobs. "I shot my dad."

Darragh raises his gun, and I tighten my hold on Lily, keeping her to my chest as he does what needs to be done. A bullet tears through Alexis' head, and she hits the ground.

Lily screams, and I keep her firmly to my chest. I let her cry for a moment. "What just happened?" She asks but doesn't look up.

I stare back at the hotel.

It's Darragh who speaks. "Alexis pulled a gun on me, and I shot her."

We stop walking, and Lily shakes her head.

"She loved your father, and she wanted someone to die." Darragh is smart at how he is wording everything. Alexis never had a weapon.

Darragh leans in close to Lily while I still have my arm around her. "Your dad asked Alexis to plant a bomb here; can you imagine how many people could have died? But Alexis saw her mistake and rushed out with the bomb."

Lily frowns, but I squeeze her arm, and she looks up at me. "Hear him out."

She swallows. I have no idea how much she is taking in, but she needs to get her story straight before we clean up the scene and ring this in.

"Mike shot her for her betrayal and then attempted to shoot me, so I fired in self-defense."

"I won't incriminate you, Darragh. I'll say I took the shot in self-defense."

Darragh lights a smoke and grins. "I've done this a few times. I'm good."

I didn't want my uncle to shoulder my responsibilities.

"Trust me; you have enough to contend with. You get Lily out of here, and I'll sort this out."

I release Lily and pull my uncle into a hug. I wasn't a hugger, but he had saved my ass.

When I turn to Lily, I know this is going to take some time for her to come to terms with but at least we could be together now.

We could finally start living.

CHAPTER TWENTY-FIVE

O'REAGAN
AN CHLANN

LILY

It's been two months since my father's funeral. Two months of coming to terms with killing him without really getting to know him as a father and not my uncle. Yet, we did spend a great deal of time together when I was a kid. He would take me shooting crows; that's how I knew how to handle Darragh's gun.

My stomach twists every time I think of what I did. I never thought I'd have the ability to take a life. But, seeing Daniel lying on the ground and watching bullets miss his head was all it took.

Hands wrap around my waist as I look down on a rainy Dublin. We've taken a short break to the capital, and the three days away from work and home have been nice.

"I could stay here forever." I meet Daniel's gaze in the reflection of the glass. My heart won't ever stop racing when he looks at me.

"We can extend our stay for awhile longer." He presses a kiss to my neck. My lips rise up as I turn in his arms and wrap my hands around his neck.

"I'd really like that."

Daniel presses his lips to mine. "Then that's what we are doing, but right now, what do you want to do?"

I already know what he has in mind, but I like to drag it out. "I..." I untangle myself from him and walk away from the large windows. "Am thinking about..." I pull my beige sweater over my head and let it float to the floor. "Going for a ...." I grin. "Bath." I run as Daniel chases me.

I'm airborne as he drags me to his chest and places hot kisses on my neck. "You are never getting away from me again, Lily McGuiness."

I wrap my arms around his neck. "You promise, Daniel O'Reagan?"

His face becomes serious, and he leans his forward against mine. "On my life."

I inhale his words, and they nestle in my soul as he carries me into the bathroom and joins me for a warm bath.

It's our second chance at something good, and this time, no one will take me from him.

THE END

I hope you enjoyed *Mafia Secrets.*

Sinner's Vow, Book One in the Murphy's Mafia Made Men Series is out now!

You can download by scanning the QR Code:

Or read on for a sneak peek:

SINNER'S VOW

CHAPTER ONE

Dread drips down my spine in a slow trickle—my stomach clenches. On either side of me, doors line a long, daunting passage. Intentionally, I'm sure.

I'm positive my father revels in intimidating visitors as they shuffle toward his study at the back of the house, the ticking of the grandfather clock taunting them with each step.

The ticking that haunts me now.

For each hand movement accompanied by a tick, I'm another step closer to my doom. Father never calls me to his office for anything good. The last time he called on me, I ended up in the hands of the Bratva.

Raven, you can do this, I remind myself as I place one Jimmy-Choo-clad foot in front of the other.

A half-strangled laugh echoes back to me, and I press my lips together. Even as my fight-or-flight response kicks in, I keep moving forward.

Because, just like all the times before, I know I have no other choice.

You could run.

I shiver and grip the sides of my dress. The memory burns in my mind of what happened the last time I ran, not from my father but from my ex-husband.

I had run home to my father, pleading with him to save me from the beast of a man he'd given me to. It had been a risk, but I didn't know who else to run to. He'd put me in that situation, and I knew there was no escape unless my father granted it.

That day, my father held me as I cried bitter tears on the shoulder of his navy jacket. My sobs jolted my body, and I didn't notice him withdraw his phone, dial my husband's number, and tell my husband to come and collect his wife.

Knock, knock, knock. I've reached the dark wooden door that leads into my father's lair.

"Come in." My father isn't a man you ever keep waiting. My fingers sprawl across the door that I push open, and I step into his office. Olbas Oil tickles my senses. The white cloth handkerchief at my father's elbow is where the strong smell emanates from. My earlier breakfast curdles in my gut.

Three large chandeliers cast light down on the crown of his head. He shuffles paperwork on his mahogany desk. As my gaze travels across the bookcases that soar above my father, I find my calm by looking at a paper dove that Louise had made for him years ago. I have no idea why he kept the present from Louise, but right now, it's what I'm seeking—a moment of calm before the impending storm. I hope this time I'm strong enough to withstand the force of whatever he unleashes on me.

"Raven—"

I pull my gaze from the bookshelves and look his way. Maintaining eye contact isn't easy. His blue eyes always appear clouded, as if there's a madness lurking.

I keep my hands firm at my side, though I want to ball my fingers into fists so I don't fidget.

He gestures toward the adjacent chair. I descend into the brown leather seat before folding my hands onto my lap, waiting for the blow from his words.

He doesn't so much as blink as he leans forward and steeples his fingers on the desk. "You've won your freedom."

I release the breath I've been holding, and without being able to stop myself, I slump into the chair. My lips drag down, and my vision wavers. It's over.

Tears spill, and I'm smiling. I'm smiling with a fierce pain in my heart. God, the price I paid for my freedom had been branded into my flesh, literally. My ex-husband used his belt as his form of punishment.

"Thank you," I find myself saying through quivering lips. I'm crashing from exhaustion. I'm crashing from being relieved from an overwhelming crushing feeling. I'm free.

Free.

"Once you marry Aidan Murphy, you are free to leave this home. You can start over wherever you want."

I'm staring at the gray-peppered crown of my father's head, my vision as clear as a cloudless hot summer's day. His black fountain pen glides with fluid motions across a piece of paper.

"Excuse me?" My voice comes out strangled, pained, heartbroken.

Without flinching, he repeats his words as he continues to write. He pauses when I don't respond and glances up at me. "I need you to retrieve information from Aidan Murphy. Once you do, you have won your and Louise's freedom."

A whimper spills from my lips. The last time I extracted information from Victor, my first husband, it almost cost me my life.

"You said the last time that if I got you the information, we would be debt free." I'm speaking out of turn. I know I've crossed an invisible line even before my father looks up at me with fire in his eyes. His fist comes down with a heavy thud on the table, and I grip the arm of the chair so I don't jump.

"It helped," he grits out. "But it wasn't enough. Yes, you did well. You kept a roof over Louise's head. You say you want to give your sister a better life, but do you mean it?"

Louise. My Achilles' heel.

The information I obtained for my father gave him millions. Where did all that money go? I want to accuse him of returning to gambling, but I also value my life.

"Once you get the information from Aidan Murphy, you can leave him. Finances will be set up for you and Louise. I'd suggest you pull yourself together. Aidan Murphy may one day rule the Irish Mafia. He won't want a weak woman at his side." He returns to his work, dismissing me.

I'm so beat down that I don't at first comprehend the dismissal. When his gaze darts to mine, my brain stalls, mentally repeating his words before I rise. He has taken everything from me. I'm ready to walk away, but I can't. Not this time. I raise my head in defiance.

"No." My pulse builds to a tempo that's more fitting to a dramatic ballad grand finale. The part where the heroine dies, or the moment the hero realizes he's already lost her.

My father rises in one swift motion. He's a large man, over six feet tall, with massive hands.

"I wasn't asking, Raven."

"I don't understand." I blink tears.

His lips curl into a snarl. "You're a woman. You aren't meant to understand the ways of a man. Just get the information from Aidan Murphy, and you have your freedom." My father settles back into his chair.

"Or maybe he would prefer someone younger." My father's mouth curves into a smile. "Louise is very striking."

My stomach roils. His words should terrify me; instead, they make me want to tear the world apart. "You will not go near Louise."

My father ascends and steps around his desk with a raised hand. I fear what will come next. I've pushed too far, and I will pay the price.

The impact of the slap doesn't just burn my jaw; the force sends me sprawling to the floor. The ridges of the wooden floor dig into my palms. My hip takes the brunt of my fall.

I'm staring at the dark wood, panting and shaking. I want to get up. I want to defy him. Maybe he senses the rebellious nature in me. His fingers plunge into my hair, and my scalp burns as he forces my head back.

"Apologize."

I want to say no again, but as his gaze fills with brutality, I know this will end with me injured and still shipped away to marry a stranger. But, for one moment, it's brief. My defiance feels so good.

"No." My heart palpitates as I try to crawl away from my father before he can unleash his wrath upon me. The abrupt opening of his study door stops his assault.

My face continues to burn from the slap he planted on my cheek. I take in shiny black shoes before traveling my gaze up black slacks all the way to George's green eyes. My bodyguard isn't looking at me. A muscle tics in his square jaw.

George captures my father's attention. "I do apologize, Mr. Collins." He glances at his wristwatch. "I'm here to collect Miss Raven. The car is waiting."

My lungs constrict painfully. No one walks into my father's office unannounced, and George follows the rules. So why did he enter without knocking? Or did he knock, and I just didn't hear the sound?

I push off the floor. My arms tremble as if I'd been lifting weights.

"Get up," my father barks as he returns to his seat behind his desk. I hate him. I hate him so much. As I stand, my tongue flicks out, licking the blood off my lips.

When I'm upright, my father pins me with a stare. "The car can wait. Have one of the servants clean her up first," he says to George without taking his beady eyes off me.

My heartbeat thump, thump, thumps. George said the car is waiting. Am I leaving right now?

"Miss Raven." George's brash words have me pivoting toward him.

"I hope you show Mr. Murphy more respect. I'm sure his hand would be far heavier than mine."

I hunch my shoulders at my father's words. I want to rebel. I want to tell him I hate him, but I place one foot in front of the other until I pass George. The office door closes as George falls into step behind me. We walk down the long corridor, and I wrap my arms around my waist to try to shake off the growing fear.

"You shouldn't antagonize him," George whispers.

I take a peek at the forty-year-old man who has never spoken to me. I wonder how long he had been standing outside my father's office door. Responding would be pointless. George steps in front of me as we enter the ornate foyer of the house. We walk past the enormous staircase to the first floor, where I sleep. I'm looking around for my sister. I want to check on her, but no one is in sight to even ask about her.

When we reach my bedroom, George opens the door but doesn't enter. No one is permitted into our sleeping quarters. I had a hand in designing my room. The gold leaf that adorns all the matching white French furniture pulls the room together. It's a mix of contemporary and old world. The large black chandelier over my bed sends light dancing across the gray silk duvet. I find my gaze ping-ponging around the luxurious space. It's my haven, where I seek solitude on the hard days. I often thrash out my pain in my quarters and try to heal myself by decorating the space. I won't return here. I shake off the sense of loss and walk to my open closet.

I need to pack. My stomach squirms in pain, and I scramble for my calm, which in this moment, I can't find. I'm leaving again to marry yet another man. Will he hurt me as Victor had? A part of me wants to curl up and find a corner to hide in. I want to bury my head and let the time pass.

But gathering some possessions and saying goodbye to Louise spurs me to my walk-in wardrobe. I freeze as George greets my father on the landing. My dread grows as I spin around, fearing he's come to finish what he started in his office.

My father barges into my room and slams my bedroom door behind him. When he spins the lock, I know it's to keep George from interfering with whatever is about to come next.

I won't have anyone to save me this time.

Download and read by scanning the QR code:

THE END

OTHER BOOKS BY VI CARTER

<u>THE CELLS OF KALASHOV</u>

THE COLLECTOR #1

THE SIXTH #2

THE HANDLER #3

<u>MURPHY'S MAFIA MADE MEN</u>

SINNER'S VOW #1

SAVAGE MARRIAGE #2

SCANDALOUS PLEDGE #3

<u>SONS OF THE MAFIA</u>

SINS OF THE MAFIA #0.5

VENGEANCE IN BLOOD #1

<u>YOUNG IRISH REBELS SERIES</u>

MAFIA PRINCE #1

MAFIA KING #2

MAFIA GAMES #3

MAFIA BOSS #4

MAFIA SECRETS #5 (NOVELLA)

<u>WILD IRISH SERIES</u>

FATHER (PREQUEL)

VICIOUS #1

RECKLESS #2

RUTHLESS #3

FEARLESS #4

HEARTLESS #5

THE BOYNE CLUB

DARK #1

DARKER # 2

DARKEST #3

PITCH BLACK #4

THE OBSESSED DUET

A DEADLY OBSESSION #1

A CRUEL CONFESSION #2

BROKEN PEOPLE DUET

BREAK ME #1

SAVE ME #2

ABOUT THE AUTHOR

Vi Carter - the queen of **DARK ROMANCE**, the mistress of suspense, and the high priestess of *PLOT TWISTS*!

When she's not busy crafting tales of the **MAFIA** that'll leave you on the edge of your seat, you can find her baking up a storm, exploring the gorgeous Irish countryside, or spending time with her three little girls.

Vi's Young Irish Rebels series has been praised by readers and can be found in English, Dutch, German, Audible and soon will be available in French.

And let's not forget her two greatest loves: ***coffee and chocolate***. If you ever need to bribe her, just offer up a mug of coffee and a slab of chocolate, and she'll be putty in your hands.

So, if you're ready to join Vi on a wild journey with the mafia, sign up for her newsletter and score a free book! Just be warned - her stories are so **ADDICTIVE**, you might not be able to put them down.

WHAT READERS ARE SAYING

Editorial Reviews

"Vi Carter has once again blown my mind with another outstanding story. She never fails to create a masterpiece with memorable characters that leap off the page. This book is complete perfection."- USA Today Bestselling Author Khardine Gray

Vi is one of those authors who never disappoints. She weaves **LOVE** & **DANGER** effortlessly. ★★★★★ stars

I definitely recommend this book. It is **SUSPENSEFUL** and exciting. I enjoy reading Vi Carter's book. ★★★★★ stars

HOW TO KEEP IN TOUCH WITH VI CARTER

Visit Vi's website: https://author-vicarter.com/

Join her newsletter: t.ly/yZWbX

Or scan the QR code:

On Facebook, Instagram, TikTok and Youtube @darkauthorvicarter and on Twitter @authorvicarter

Or scan the QR code:

ACKNOWLEDGEMENTS

I'm very lucky to have such amazing readers and Beta Readers. I want to thank the following people who worked with me on this book.

Developmental Editor: Amanda Cuff

Editor: Sherry Schafer

Proofreader: Michele Rolfe

Blurb was written by: Tami Thomason

Beta Readers

Amanda Sheridan

Lucy Korth

Tami Thomason

Printed in Dunstable, United Kingdom

65841510R00080